The Lives & Deaths of Morbius Mozella

Stephen Mosley

THE LIVES & DEATHS OF MORBIUS MOZELLA

Copyright © Stephen Mosley 2021

MORBIUS MOZELLA and all related characters and elements copyright © Stephen Mosley 2021

All rights reserved. This book or any portion thereof may not be reproduced or used in any manner whatsoever without the express written permission of the author except for the brief use of quotations in a book review.

Author photograph copyright © Ellie Rodriguez 2019

Cover design and inside illustration copyright © Anthony Farren 2020

www.stephenmosley.net

ISBN: 979-8-7214-0170-1

ONE

Hollywood, 1967.

Tinseltown takes little notice of the skull-faced man in dark cape and evening clothes; there are plenty of kooks along the Boulevard today.

Morbius Mozella always walks to work. The studio is not far from home, though it is far from a studio: A dilapidated concrete block somewhere near Santa Monica, drunks and tourists stagger past this unremarkable building unaware that, inside, one of Hollywood's once-great stars is preparing his latest scene. And one of Hollywood's leading comedians is getting ready to scupper it.

Benny Miller is television's hottest draw right now. Every night, millions of Americans tune into his show, the creatively titled *Benny Miller Show*, and laugh collectively at his various catchphrases, the most popular being: "Say, that's some haircut you got there!" This is a cry that rings out in every schoolyard the day after the show is aired. The comedian is destined to repeat such phrases—on talk shows, in tuxedos, at awards ceremonies—to gleeful applause and shared hilarity for the rest of his days. Though no one ever knows why they are laughing. But even the old folks think Benny is a hoot.

Morbius Mozella remembers the great comedians, and reprising one of his famous vampire roles for the low-budget movie debut of this catchphrase-spouting clown was never part of his dream.

America's leading comic is holding things up. Right now, he's talking to the director, a fifteen-year-old genius, whose sole line of direction is: "Was that supposed to be scary? I didn't find it funny."

"This script is garbage!" yells Miller. The director merely blinks at him. A small group of people, with mouths to feed and homes to maintain, huddle behind giant cameras: Whirring, one-eyed monsters, they look far more threatening than when the great Mozella last faced such gizmos.

"Let's roll," says the director, finally.

Miller strides to the set; Mozella strolls behind, cape quietly flapping.

Thought used to go into sets like these. This one is covered with cobwebs, concealing its cardboard flaws. Slipping on a rubber spider, Miller gets tangled in a stringy web. "Yuck! What is this stuff?"

"Places, everyone," a voice sounds from behind those cyclopic machines: "And . . . action!"

Sharona Charlot, the leading lady, is interrupting a mildly lucrative career in nudie musicals to make this feature, so it's best to get it right. In diaphanous nightgown, she prowls the cobwebbed, cardboard set. Large grey squares are painted along the sides. They are supposed to resemble stony castle walls. They resemble large grey squares. Mozella leaps out of the darkness, cape outspread and fangs flashing.

"uuurrgh," says the leading lady (it says "AAAAAAARRRRRGGGHH!" in the script.)

The director doesn't flinch; just sits there, mute, behind the camera, a human toadstool.

Mozella secretes the screaming, petrified (unconcerned, bad) actress behind his cloak as he lowers his fangs to her silken throat. Suddenly, he is knocked aside, a little too roughly, by the nation's top comedy act. Mozella flops to the floor. A thousand fake cobwebs shudder. Four thin, painted walls collapse.

"Say," the funnyman yelps: "That's some haircut you got there!"

"Cut!"

Nobody is laughing. Miller looks to the director with wide eyes searching for approval. The director looks towards Mozella; Sharona is helping him up.

"Say, Mozella," says the director, chewing a fresh wad of gum taken without asking from the soundman. "Was that supposed to be scary?"

Mozella looks at him blankly.

"And what was that business with the cloak?" The director wraps his arms around a stunned Sharona, concealing her and illustrating his point. "I want to see your teeth sink in. I want to see you bite her."

"eeuw," says Sharona, with slightly more emotion than when the eye of the whirring monster was upon her.

The director nods at Mozella for a while, before scuttling back behind his camera. "Okay. Places, everyone. Let's take it from the top."

The starlet grumbles. Technicians rebuild the set. The director fiddles with the camera.

"Hey!" says a voice. *"Hey!"*

It is Miller.

The director looks up as if awoken from deep slumber.

"How was *I*?" Patting his chest with squat fingers, the comic looks like a desperate toad.

The director gapes at his star as if he's trying to remember who he is. "Oh," he says, eventually:

"You were fine."

Miller rolls his eyes and steps back to the shadows. He'll say the line louder next time, and knock Mozella harder to the floor.

"Action!"

Sharona Charlot wanders around the set looking tired; she can get better money elsewhere. Mozella leaps out and seizes her throat.

"uuh," the starlet emotes.

Despite the director's wishes, Mozella shields his victim with his cloak, and sinks his head slowly, menacingly, beneath it. He's been doing it this way for years.

Within the cape's scarlet lining, he notices that the young lady is looking puzzled, wondering why it has suddenly gone dark.

"Say!"

Mozella feels a burly comedian push him over. He lands hard against the studio floor, the breath shooting from his lungs.

"That's some haircut you got there!"

"Cut! Print it! That's a wrap!"

When Mozella looks up, the leading lady has already left the set. Miller struts away, looking very pleased with himself. The director is standing over the ageing horror star.

"Uh, Mozella," he says, without looking at his subject: "Was that supposed to be funny? I didn't find it scary."

At the side of the stage, beyond the hot lights, Sharona Charlot chats with Benny Miller. "Hey, pal!" the funnyman cracks to an unsmiling gaffer: "Easy on the mayo!" This is another of his catchphrases, and although Sharona unleashes a braying laugh, her pretty eyes never smile.

TWO

It scrapes at the window, spat from the dark.

She lies on warm sheets, in the clinch of his shadow.

Moving with a cautious glide, his garments, soiled with graveyard dust, traipse the chamber floor.

He's locked in her warmth, yet utterly cold, crippled to the guts like a boy with desire.

He approaches her with sad-eyed longing.

Overcome by purpose, he scoops her soft body into his gnarled arms.

Drawing back lips that ache for a kiss, long teeth sink into lily neck. A hot surge of blood hits his mouth.

It's not the touch that he's yearned for, but addiction is sated. Damp eyes look Heavenward, filling with shame.

He must drink and gorge until her body is drained; until he's taken from her all that he can: He who has nothing of himself to give.

When her sighs finally fade, too sudden, too soon, she lies limp, white and gone in the stain of his shadow.

He cannot avoid himself and all that he is. And she's lost to the chill of his hold yet again.

Morbius Mozella is watching his old films. These

black-and-white worlds are the lands of his prime, yet he returns to them with bittersweet feeling. Memories, those awkward ghosts, dance across the screen, as tears crawl down his skull-like face. Between sips of gin, he threads more reels in the dust-lit machine.

Within rain-lashed walls, a dank enclosure, where the Scientist tends to the Thing on the table.

His exhausted nerve creeps close to shatters. Oily blobs of shadow fill the hollows of his cracked and grinning face.

A lightning-flash illuminates the Thing, as it slowly twitches to life.

Rising and stumbling to an awkward birth, low groans issue from black, shrivelled lips.

Its long, grey limbs grope for understanding; sad eyes loll like a failing child.

Then, enter the Girl; her own eyes slick with hope — until the Thing places fingers about pretty neck, and life is gone from her as swift as it was stitched in him.

In this dust-speckled tomb, the Scientist stands alone, despondent as the corpse-grey walls; as dead inside as the Thing he has made, and the Girl he still loves, and should have loved better.

These worlds lie lost inside him; crowded with phantoms; swollen with ghosts; crawling forth, exposing his shadow. He pours another gin and toasts his wife. She lies pale and upright in the furthest corner, in the soft satin lining of her box.

The moon, no longer swathed in cloud, bears melancholy witness to the Beast who tramples fog-sheathed grounds; prowling with pitiful, drooling eyes, where once she was captive.

Those eyes are no longer his; they're no longer hers.

He is gone like the touch of his hand: She would shred like tissue to his current caress.

There is only the Beast, with alien drive, and the quivering pulp of torn throats asunder.

The entire Town is one torn and twitching throat.

She fills with silver what was once filled with her; dimming all flames she lit on the way.

She sees him again, as he once was, and how he will always be in her thoughts: Shrouded in death with the peace that life owed.

The Town sways with relief. It's over, this curse, but in the safety of dreams; and she walks back alone, beneath that gloating full moon.

When the movie's over, fading into one with the rest

of the gloom, he sits still awhile in the belly of darkness. The projector whirs, a dying growl; an appropriate sound to the black. He lies beside her, eyes wide and searching, in hideous rehearsal for that one joyous day when Death shall find all that is lost, and ferry it safely, back to her arms.

THREE

Morbius Mozella is my name. Some of you may recall
That on your screens, a few years ago, my face was on them all.
Those movies you thrilled to so late at night that caused you to grow chill,
Mostly starred yours truly—'twas my name atop the bill.
I played all your favourite monsters, the ones that made you scream;
I starred in all those late-night thoughts of yours too scary to call dreams.
Recall my fiendish antics, my evil doings in the night
All performed by me, my friends, in artistic black-and-white
Remember haunted castles, ghouls and phantoms, rubber bats;
Remember screaming maidens dipped in pits of boiling wax.
Remember good old Horror as it was back in the day,
Before the creeps and psychopaths hacked my

cobwebbed dreams away.

For now the world's more tortured than all my female leads,

And a good old-fashioned fright film is what this sad Earth needs.

So here I'm back, with torture rack, and token companion hunchback;

To give the world one chance to feel a shock and fear that isn't real.

(Poem penned by Morbius Mozella to help publicize his ever-threatened comeback.)

FOUR

Surrounded by darkness; in the tarry pit of a dream.

His chest tightens; his brow perspires.

Angular grey juts emerge, sculpted from the big black nothing, where familiar voices garble.

"Okay, Morbius. Next scene."

It is the voice of Max.

His old friend steps forward, as sculptured and grey as the shadows around them.

"You know what to do, Morbius."

It is not a question. Morbius nods, assured, and steps into the laboratory. Several carefully placed lamps throw artful shadows along the dusty shelved rows of strange apparatus. Mozella stands amidst it all, alien to the world, yet authentic to his own: He melts into the surroundings.

"Action."

Raising the beaker to his lips, he peers cautiously. Only the shadows are in on his secret.

Suddenly, he tips the bubbling fluid down his throat. A placid calm coats him, until . . .

Eyes roll back in a slackened face. His body contorts in furious jolts, like a compound of living things all scurrying at once, jarring to be free.

He throws himself into a confused pile, before straightening and slouching and hobbling and grinning and leering and scuttling and becoming somebody else. Something else.

"Cut."

Light streams down, razing the dark. They are clapping their hands and smiling warm smiles. Even Max is smiling: A smile as wide and curled as his waxed moustache. He places an arm about the transformed man, now resembling his star. Everyone is happy, just for one moment.

Mozella wakes into a humid silence.

And all of his friends have gone.

FIVE

Beyond the dust-fogged smudge of this ruined abode, Hollywood lies in wait: A slumbering sea-beast that roars out dashed hopes; the sun veils the horrors of its proffered joys. This deceptive light fawns at the windows, begging to intrude.

Morbius Mozella steps gently from his casket like a shadow extended, mourning poor lost Elizabeth, who will never step from her casket again. He dusts himself off, peering through the viscous gloom. Lighting a candle, he winces from its faint illumination, then clambers about his home like a graceful spider.

The interiors resemble the crumbling refuge of a miniature ransacked church. Every surface is plastered with cobwebs. The broken limbs of a dying tree crawl up a solitary window, throwing jagged shadows over a small wooden desk. Within a feathery mass of dust, there lies a book: The unfinished memoirs of Mozella.

An uncomfortable old throne is the sole embellishment of the chamber's centre. It lies facing the blank screen on which he projects nightly his monochrome past and ephemeral glories.

Elizabeth lies propped against the furthest wall, in a sarcophagus (his & hers). Dark eyes staring from behind black lashes, she's a radiant, yet vacant doll.

In another shady spot sits the harmonium, its bone-white keys swept clean of dust from his nightly serenades to departed love.

He hopes the mournful rhapsodies reach her in her slumbers, where she waits to be awoken by some long-promised kiss. Aching to join her, wherever she has drifted, he prays significantly for that glorious day.

All that remains is her body: A divine tenement, severed from all shades of sorrow and mirth.

A rumpled cape lies over the throne like a shadow made of cloth. Blowing off the dust, he throws it on his shoulders and kisses his wife goodbye. It is time to go to work.

SIX

"Was that supposed to be scary?"

Mozella lies scrunched in the plastic coffin. Benny Miller heaves a plastic stake into the actor's armpit. It hurts like hell. But Mozella never complains.

Sharona Charlot screams: "eaurgh."

The small bearded man in glasses, who hides beneath the plastic coffin, belatedly releases a jet of fake blood through a complex pump contraption that looks like it was constructed by a lazy child. The blood hits Miller's face for the second time that afternoon. *"For Christ's sakes!"* he 'ad-libs' through wobbling lips.

The men behind the rolling cameras bury their heads in silent joy as Miller stumbles around the set, cursing. He resembles a man in an ape suit rampaging across a cardboard Tokyo. The bloated comic suddenly remembers that there are microphones encircling him and composes himself for his next line. Dipping a finger into the blood on his face, he sucks it off with a loud smack. "Hmm," he grins like an idiot: "Tastes like ketchup!" This just happens to be another of his famous catchphrases.

"Okay, cut!"

"You bastards! You scheming sons of bitches!" Miller clutches his scorched gullet, red sauce dripping from his jowls. Sharona Charlot, dead eyes in vibrant satin, looks shocked. Mozella stays in his coffin, pretending to be dead. The crew are all laughing: The director has replaced the ketchup blood with a foul mixture of hot sauces concocted over lunch. The joke hasn't satisfied him as he thought it would, though. He can barely raise a smile as Miller's throat burns. Still, his bearded lackeys are falling about, killing themselves with laughter.

"You bastards!" Everyone watches in silence as the comic repeats this unscripted line until his cries grow hoarse.

"Okay," says the director: "Can we take it from the top? It wasn't funny enough."

"And I was a bit late with the sauce," a small bearded voice pipes in from below the plastic coffin.

In a flash of inspiration, the director offers some direction: "Uh, Mozella, can you be funnier this time? Okay, let's roll."

Everyone reluctantly complies. But first, they have to wait for a small bearded woman to wipe the sauce off Mozella's cape. As this is happening, he notices a large shadowy man waiting around on set, dressed in attire very similar to his. *Perhaps a deranged fan?* Mozella thinks assuredly, sinking half-clean into his box.

Before the director can scream *"Action!"* a small bearded man, whom no one's ever seen before, marches onto the set. It's the producer. He's waving a copy of the script in his hand. *"This picture needs more sex!"* he postures like a let-down toddler.

"Okay," the director nods. "Uh, Mozella, you can go home now."

The small bearded woman with the sauce-stained handkerchief helps Mozella out of his coffin, and the tall shadowy figure who's dressed like Mozella climbs in.

"Let's shoot the 'Continental' scene," the director chirps.

Benny Miller rubs his hands together. Small bearded men help Sharona out of her nightgown.

Morbius Mozella doesn't know what's going on, but he shudders, as the small bearded woman leads him off the set.

SEVEN

Studio publicity biography of Morbius Mozella, written and circulated at the height of the actor's fame, circa 1934.

Morbius Mozella has hit the heights of Horror in numerous gruesome performances of recent memory, making him the world's number-one "horror star" and rightly so, as the man himself was born and raised in that land of howling phantoms, Transylvania, where legends of werewolves and vampires still run rife among the locals. It is memories of such folktales that inspired Mozella to become the leading connoisseur of all things ghastly and supernatural. But this quiet man of mystery could not be further removed from the parts he portrays onscreen: It may surprise the film-fan to know that Morbius Mozella is happier at home with a good book, than prowling the dark in search of pretty victims! He arrived in America, dreaming of stardom, without a dime to his name, but it wasn't long before this distinguished European gentleman came to the notice of Hollywood, where his unique brand of stylized menace has been much appreciated by audiences, if not critics. We hope Mozella continues bringing life to his grotesque gallery of fiends for many bump-ridden nights to come.

EIGHT

*Extract from the London **Times**, December 28th, 1895.*

On the Eve of Christmas, the small Yorkshire town of Burlham was invaded by an unusually large flock of ravens, flying in formation.

According to one bystander, Yuletide revellers heard "an unholy screeching" coming from above. Looking up, they saw that the night sky was blackened further by "at least a thousand" birds.

Onlookers also reported that an object "rather like a baby" could be seen dangling from one of the ravens' beaks. "They dropped it onto the moors," another witness tells us: "And then they flew off."

Perhaps it's worth remembering that, in this time of good cheer, the taverns of Burlham are rarely empty and many 'arfs are swizzled. As for the birds and their "foundling", nothing has been seen of them since.

NINE

*Excerpt from the unpublished memoirs of Morbius Mozella, written at his Hollywood home in 1967, whilst waiting to be called back onto the set of **Benny Miller vs the Vampire Man**.*

I came into this world under the name of Felix Francis on the Eve of Christmas 1895. The part of the world that greeted me on arrival from the forgotten warmth of my mother's womb was the small town of Burlham, Yorkshire, England.

Burlham was a place of rolling countryside, narrow roads and perpetual winters. The land was sliced by a winding, silver river, segregating the village into two areas: One poor, the other only slightly more affluent. There was no question as to which side of the river my family and I lived.

My mother was a quiet woman of ethereal presence. My father held a much more fearsome countenance. He was a large man with black eyes and beard who shouted, bullied and bellowed his way through life, hammering curses and obscenities at anything that crossed his path. I was scared of him. And so, too, I imagine, was Mother. I stayed out of his way as best I could; not easy in a house with only three small rooms: A sparse living area downstairs, which also served as a kitchen and bathroom, owing to a small stove in one corner, and a large tin bucket in the other. There were two tiny bedrooms upstairs for my parents and I respectively. There was also a cellar, but I never dared venture down there. It was full of bats. Our toilet was outside, in the street.

My earliest memories are violent ones; receiving heavy thrashings from my father for some petty, unremembered misdeed, as my mother stood idly by, watching. During these moments, Father often told me that Mother had found me on the moors when I was a baby. "I wish she'd never brought you home," he'd say. "An ugly thing like you deserves to be abandoned." Whether it was true or not, I certainly felt like I didn't belong.

I took to staying away from home as much as I could, aware that there was an almost tangible sadness haunting its walls. I tried everything to escape that feeling, but the surrounding hillsides made me feel just as trapped. Only by retreating into my imagination, did I discover a world of understanding.

My fantasies were fuelled by an important discovery: One day, with a newfound sense of chivalry or foolishness, I explored my father's room when he was away at work. In a dusty corner by his bed, I found piles of books, which I surreptitiously devoured, borrowing one at a time whenever Father was out. Concealing them beneath the loose floorboards of my room, I would tuck the precious tomes into my trousers to enjoy on excursions. My father never noticed they were missing.

I found comfort in the works of great authors and poets: Shelley, Hugo, Stevenson, Doyle, Poe, Dumas, Dickens, Maupassant, Bierce, Hawthorne, Irving, Wells, and three sweet girls from nearby Haworth, who went by the name of Brontë. I read them all, developing an especially keen interest on fictions that were geared towards the macabre or fantastic; anything that offered a view differing from my own. My father was a fierce man, but his heart seemed to soften, like my own, to the minds of Heavenly creation.

I gave in to playacting long before I knew such a thing existed, enacting stories plucked from my head, inspired by worlds in other heads, more celebrated than my own. I would assume the identities of all the characters in my little plays, running through the village, speaking their lines aloud, and making life up as I went along. On any given day, I could be a pirate, pillaging the country lanes; a musketeer, rescuing illusory damsels in the woodland; a detective, scouring the moorland for clues; or one of Poe's tortured souls, wandering forlorn across the valley. Should someone happen to pass my way . . . well, I was used to funny looks.

Fortunately, Burlham was a town with many lonely places. I emoted my little stories to an audience of one (myself), believing I was flawed or insane, but knowing no other way to live. (And this is how I continue to live, some seventy years later.)

When neighbouring children ran and kicked balls in the dirt outside, I preferred to stay inside, dreaming, reading, acting, writing or drawing. (I had now begun to write and illustrate my adventures in styles inspired by my heroes.) Sometimes my mother would break her strange silence by softly encouraging me to play alongside the other children. Forced outside by Mother's will, I found myself standing awkwardly alone at one end of the road, whilst my peers played effortlessly in groups at the other end. I continued to play in my own world. It was the only way that made sense to me.

Then there came an intrusion called school. I couldn't understand why I was suddenly dragged from my imaginary existence and placed in this very real hovel with larger groups of children who integrated with an apparent ease that, again, seemed utterly alien to me. I felt more awkward and alone than ever in this sterile environment; always afraid that I would do something wrong, and be punished yet again by the stern-faced woman who barked orders at us from the front of the class. She tried to teach us to read, but I had already learnt. She expected us to know nonsensical puzzles involving numbers, which seemed beyond any reasonable comprehension. I was constantly at odds, though my intentions were good. Seeing other children place gifts of rosy red apples on the teacher's desk, I decided to emulate their gesture: The teacher was not amused, though, when I crushed a mouldy grey pumpkin into her hands. From that day until this, I loathed enforced education. I have always believed that if a human being wants to know something, they can go out and learn it for themselves; we hold more knowledge than they would ever have us believe.

I looked as unusual as I felt. As if my insides were out for all to see. Everyone took to calling me

"Skullface". (A nickname appropriated to "Scaryface" in my later years, and apportioned to me not by indifferent children, but by the movie-going public, in what I'd like to think was reverence.) I felt ugly and useless—a guileless little thing. Even my father would withdraw his hand immediately from my face after striking it; as one would refrain from touching a poisonous reptile. I took to clasping my hands over my strange countenance, observing the world through fingers. My teacher encouraged me to put my fingers to better use in my schoolwork, then placed a sack over my offending features. I could see them through the jagged eyeholes, laughing and sneering; I could smell their indifference through the rotten, musty stench that clung to the insides of the sack. For the first twenty or so years of my life, I lived enclosed; my soul silently crumbling in the Hessian prison.

I spent most of my later school days in absentia, preferring to compose poetry on the sloping riverbanks. Although I was initially punished for my AWOL stance, my wanderings gradually went unnoticed. I was something of an absent ghost, rarely haunting the ominous classroom.

I daydreamed my way through school, leaving it behind as an unpleasant, humiliating memory. But from that intrusion, I was forced into another, as if my life rotated on some grim carousel.

I was twelve when I started work at the machine shop: That horrible place of ugly machinery; still whirring in my mind as robust monsters against a glowering backdrop. Initially, I slaved there afternoons only, attending school in the mornings. "Out of the frying pan, into the fire" is a simple, but deft way to describe those days. From the age of fourteen, I was working there full-time, and would continue to do so sporadically for the next four or so years.

These industrial workhouses began jutting from the landscapes on which I told my stories. I never questioned what they were back then; just supposed them to be yet another disturbance to my secluded lifestyle. I never apprehended that I would, one day, be forced to slave away inside them, and that would be the future I ached for so impossibly.

The stench of sweat in those places was overpowering. Hundreds of poor souls perspired in there for paltry gains, and did so without question for the rest of their days. My father worked in such a mill, though never daring to speak to him, I never knew exactly what he did for a living, suffice to say that it didn't earn him much of one; but I was probably following in his grim footsteps, just as every child did with a father to follow. I existed in a somnambulistic state, never fully aware of my surroundings, performing my work in a perfunctory daze.

During the day, I worked those damnable machines with robotic regulation, ignorant as to what grand labour, if any, my efforts amounted to; ever fearful that I could lose my fingers in the grinding metal cogs. I would need those fingers for my evenings when I painted and read, creating landscapes prettier than I beheld, and dreaming of occupying them some revered day.

In search of a life outside my own, I began furthering my solitary travels, via the railroads that now stretched across the countryside. Thus, I discovered a slew of larger cities beyond the village. On drifting these unfamiliar streets, I became aware of grand buildings; inside which, people dreamt as I did, without feeling wrong for who they were. These buildings were called theatres, and my discovery of them heralded the first impressions that I was, after all, not alone on this Earth.

By the time I realised that life *did* have meaning concealed about its darkness, God sent more disorder crashing down to my existence. And He'd garbed the latest in the destructive styles of Death and War.

TEN

The unpublished memoirs of Mozella continue.

In hindsight, I can attribute Mother's strange silence to disease, though I was much too young to be aware of this at the time. She grew stranger, and thus more silent, until, one day, she was no longer there. It felt like she'd faded into the near-tangible sadness that made-up our home.

I caught my father weeping as violently as he performed any other action, and, on beholding this, found myself feeling tangled inside, not really knowing what to think. But when I escaped to the hills outside and clambered over the hard, grey rocks, I felt my eyes moisten like that stone, and knew I would never see her again.

Life was harder with Mother gone. I would come home from the factory and retire immediately to my room, bathing my tired eyes in some treasured new tome I had afforded with the monthly wage. Father would arrive home a little later and retire to his room. We never spoke, at least I never to him, but sometimes he would level some criticism at me regarding the way I dressed, spoke or looked. Other times, he would angrily berate me for misplacing a book or utensil he had lost himself. We were both too old for the robust thrashings of my childhood, but I still rarely left the house without a heavy, paternal hand clouting its way across my sack-encased head. There was never any reason for such unpleasantness. Unpleasantness is always unreasoned. Blazing rows had become more frequent, and I was forced further from home. We couldn't co-exist.

I began to spend more time in the city of Fordley, some twenty-odd miles east of Burlham, often forsaking my duties at the workplace with the same insouciance I had displayed at school. I would wander the lamp-lit streets, gawping with wide-eyed innocence at the gorgeous displays of galleries, museums and concert halls. It was in the latter that I indulged my passion for music, taking in blissful interpretations of Beethoven and J.S. Bach (whose composition "Sheep May Safely Graze" remains my favourite work).

These sojourns still burn bright in my memory's eye. The earliest motorcars chugged along the roads as a whole array of people dashed about.

I would observe and listen to these characters,

noting accents, movements and idiosyncrasies. They fascinated me. I would sit silently sketching them on some uncomfortable bench in the square, or in a park, observing how utterly oblivious they seemed to their environment, relating to one another with an air I had never previously encountered. Conversely, the people of Burlham were as strange and silent as my mother had been, and with the strong exception of my father, tended to keep themselves to themselves. Of much more interest, however, were those who related to each other in the theatres I began to frequent with ever-growing fervour.

I had seen things like it only in dreams. Here, souls seemed to soar free across the darkened stage; free from the wretched lumps of flesh that housed them; free of the imprisoning rituals that life forces us to perform daily until we die. For two hours at a time, I was free of all this.

Sitting in silent worship, I idolised all those involved in conjuring these dramatic enchantments, and, thus, I ached to join them, to be part of this more legitimate world of make-believe. It differed from my own in that this world actually incited emotional responses from those that it played to, whereas, I had always played alone to the roaring winds. I understood the reaction of the audience as I felt it too, in a rare instance of shared emotion. And if I could make others feel that way, then my life would have purpose.

On viewing the famed Shakespearean actor and tragedian Sir Hubert Hearthwright on one of his popular tours of the provinces, my soul was irrevocably gripped. He became my idol. His bellowing, baroque method impressed upon me a style that was so much larger than life, and thus twice as arresting. I perceived a light to my recurrent gloom. This was what I had been searching for all those years, lost among the Burlham hills.

I even sent Sir Hubert a "fan letter", eliciting how thankful I was for his work. When I received a signed photograph of the man himself, some months later, it was the proudest moment of my life thus far; an item I still treasure.

Hearthwright's roles, which had a leaning towards the malformed and demonic (so much more interesting than the surface of everyday folk) etched themselves to my soul. I poured all my carefully hoarded gains into following the great man and his contemporaries across the country, absorbing their portrayals at every stop.

I saw him one Christmas in *Peter Pan*, rampaging across the stage so gracefully as Captain Hook.

Swinging his dreaded hook at the crowd, he was indeed a frightening apparition, but in a way that encouraged giggles of relief after the initial shivers. This was entertainment of the highest order, and what's more, an escape route from my unhallowed life. Raised above the secretive walls of my dreams, I could now see a world beyond.

I knew it was implausible that I should join the esteemed ranks of Sir Hubert's team of professional players, but I became aware of smaller amateur groups and repertory companies that were always looking for new talent. Could I, a lowly dreamer of lofty hopes, ever pass myself off as an actor?

Responding to an advertisement in a theatre lobby, I made my way on stammering legs to an amateur society's rented lodgings for a readthrough of *A Midsummer Night's Dream*. I was unfamiliar with the play and unwary of Shakespeare; at school, we had been forced to dissect the playwright's words as though they were biological specimens. Upon reading the play aloud with others of a like-mind, though, the words became living expressions of beauty and magic. I felt content amongst people for the first time.

The production would be put on the following March in one of Fordley's quainter venues. The flames in my belly roared too fierce for me to ignore any longer. I couldn't allow them to continue burning my insides, unfed.

ELEVEN

Hollywood, 1967. The penultimate day of filming **Benny Miller vs the Vampire Man**.

"The title of this picture had better change," says the director.

"It won't," the producer assures him.

"What's wrong with the title?" asks Benny Miller: "It says everything."

Unfortunately, he is right.

"It's a crummy title," says Sharona Charlot. "It's a crummy movie."

Unfortunately, she is right.

Sharona's not having one of her better days. It's made even worse when the small bearded creep of a producer places his hand upon her buttocks. "Asshole!" she screams as he makes his exit. The producer merely laughs.

"Okay," says the director: "Let's get to work." Everyone sighs. "Where's Morbius?"

Morbius Mozella is lying in his coffin. He has been waiting for filming to resume for the past three hours. Unfortunately, these hacks are more concerned with snorting white powder than creating great art. It wasn't like this in the old days.

"Ah, there you are." Somebody finds him. "I think he's fallen asleep!"

"Okay, Mozella," says the director: "Beauty sleep's over. Time to get back to work."

Mozella would rather be at home writing his memoirs, recording a time when he was accustomed to collaborating with real artists: People who didn't need to take drugs in order to feel creative.

"Action!"

Benny Miller and Sharona Charlot creep into the crypt. "Whew," says Miller, wiping his sweaty face: "This place sure is creepy!" Mozella rises from his coffin and hisses at them. Sharona screams. Benny yowls. "Hey, Pal," he stammers, acting slightly frightened: "Easy on the mayo!" The quivering pair run off the set. The vampire slumps back into his coffin.

"Cut. Perfect. Print it!"

"I thought that was garbage," says Miller. "I'd like to do it again."

No one is listening; they're glad it's over. The director looks at his watch. "I feel a little wiggy." He looks drugged to the eyeballs. "Does anyone have any grass?" Murmurs on set. Mozella just lies in his coffin.

"Yeah," he hears a young voice finally declare. "I got some quality shit. Let's have a party right here!"

A deafening cheer. The obnoxious drone of loud, thrashing music. The stench of putrid smoke. When Mozella finds the strength to lift his head, he sees Benny Miller snorting powder from a young girl's thighs, and Sharona Charlot writhing provocatively on a small bearded man's knee (though it might be a chimpanzee; it's hard to see through all the fumes).

There's a blur of dancing youngsters, all mingling together. "Hey, Mozella," says one of them, puffing on a fragrant joint: "Fancy a hit?" Flailing like a rubber band, the youth disappears amidst the swirling, scented mists, fusing with the noise.

Mozella shivers. The sight of humanity never fails to heave the past upwards like bile.

It's a madhouse.

It's Germany, 1917.

TWELVE

Germany, 1917.

The sky frowns down on a land ripped by battle. Within clumps of trees, like rotted stumps of broccoli, there lies the asylum: A solid stone emporium, twisting from the earth, housing those shattered by life and war.

They scurry about the hospital catacombs, immersed in private worlds like ants amongst the soil. One of them drinks invisible tea from invisible cups; another sits bent, weaving unseen cloth. Some other poor soul has a laugh like pealing thunder, which dissolves into a weep as soft as rain.

Over there, in that dark corner, stand three unwary gentlemen: One is very quiet, one has a moustache, and the other is drawing on the wall.

"The title of this picture had better change," says the man with the moustache.

"It won't," the artist assures him.

Vincent Mugle steps back from his latest masterpiece: The figure of a screaming woman scrawled in charcoal on the grainy wall.

"What is the title again?" says moustache man.

"It's called 'Screaming Lady'," the artist responds, not for the first time.

"In that case, I take back everything I said earlier. The title's perfect. Don't change it."

"Splendid," says the artist. "I'm glad you agree."

Vincent Mugle is a starving French artist, fond of rotten leaves, who is more partial to charcoal than war. Men are simple beings who fight to be complex; he is a simple being who knows what he likes. If only the rest of the world could deal with their problems in the quiet, harmless manner he deals with his own; confining them to a canvas, or an asylum wall; painted worlds that can be revisited within an eyeball's flicker. When others viewed these worlds, and heard the artist expound his views, they locked him in the asylum as fast as they could.

The other gentleman, Max Spurning, is German. His carefully waxed moustache sits upon a head that often shakes in dismay. Objecting to war, he prefers drinking to fighting (he prefers it to most other things, too). A few beers make everyone equal, he'd always thought, so let's just get drunk and pretend that we love each other. It was thoughts like this that had brought him to the asylum.

No one really knows the third gentleman, the silent one. He was dragged in here quite peacefully, claiming, in a quiet fashion, to be: "Demetrius; betrothed to Hermia; Helena, I spurn." One of the madmen informed the confused orderlies that "Demetrius" is a character from a play by William Shakespeare. Assuming the new inmate to be an actor, he was promptly thrown into the asylum.

While it was true that "the actor" had been involved in amateur theatre, and had even taken part in a play by the Bard, his role in the production, according to a surviving programme, is listed as "Moth, one of the Fairies". This "Demetrius" fellow was played by someone else.

Due to our poverty of language and expression, nobody really knows who anyone is, but in the instance of "the actor" this was a good thing, because he is an Englishman. And Englishmen in First World War Germany are none too welcome. His real name, though he never speaks it, is Felix Francis. Nevertheless, the lunatics got together and christened him "Morbius Mozella". They have a name for everybody in here.

Morbius had been a soldier in France, but never knew why, believing the beginnings of a promising stage career had been broken by war. Naturally, people were curious as to how he'd ended up in a German asylum without anyone knowing he was British. The latter he achieved by the ingenious rouse of never speaking, and the former was attained by, as he put it later in his unpublished memoirs, "growing sick and tired of witnessing a surplus of brains in helmets". The soldier simply tore off his uniform, put down his gun and "wandered off": Wandered "through war-torn lands and desecrated fields, in air blackened with death, by weeping rivers, beneath bleeding skies", stumbling eventually into "enemy" Germany. They found him crouched beneath the broccoli trees, weeping insensibly by a wide, still pond, his tears rippling the mirror of a starry sky.

Everyone thought his story was unlikely when they eventually heard it, but it was the only past the stranger was prepared to offer. All they knew was that he did end up here somehow, and people had crazier truths.

.

THIRTEEN

Excerpts from the unissued memoirs of Max Spurning, film director; spoken to a tape recorder at his Hollywood home whilst waiting for death in the summer of 1956.

[. . .] so, there I was in a nuthouse in Germany. The year was 1917. I wasn't a man who made friends easily, but here I seemed to fit in. Vincent Mugle I met because he was drawing on my knees. He drew everywhere with his little black crayons that the orderlies provided for him, and as soon as I was admitted there, he was drawing on my knees. Normally I would have been quite mad (normally I was quite mad, hence being in a "madhouse"—Ha. Ha.), but as soon as I saw his depiction of little black birds on my knees, my heart melted, and we were friends since then. And besides, he had such a kindly face, at least in those bare patches of it I could see shining through his beard (which seemed to eat up his head).

We were drawn to each other because we were both artistic men with facial hair who enjoyed being thus. My greatest work of art was my moustache, which I sculpted with wax daily, so that the ends pointed up at my eyes. This later became my trademark. The orderlies were very kind here: They had no wax, but they supplied me with daily rations of "clay" for my grooming. Mugle would always steal it for use in his sculptures, which initially caused me to dribble in fury. But as soon as I spied his pretty sculptures of twisted figures, my heart melted yet again like the drooping ends of my moustache.

The director of the asylum, Herr Hoffmann, didn't have any facial hair. He was a round little man who scuttled like a beetle down the long, black corridors. He was always eating sausages, which he never offered to us, although we were so hungry.

Though the orderlies, by contrast, showed us kindness, they were also very confused: Never more so than when they brought in the man whom we now know as Morbius Mozella. He was claiming to be some great villain from Shakespeare, or some such person, and they had found him weeping by the pond. As, initially, he didn't speak much, we didn't really know what he was. Later, when he spoke, we still didn't know what he was, though he told me he was an actor, and I liked him immediately, for I had been a performer of sorts, too.

Morbius liked to wear a sack on his head, because he was hideously deformed. In truth, he looked more disfigured with the bag, and I eventually persuaded him to cast the silly sack into the pond outside. From between the bars through which we lived, we threw it out and watched it sink into the sludge and dirt. I then saw before me a beautiful man: A being of awkward grace. I had seen stranger sights in my youth to make the skull-headed man appear as nothing more than a rash below the eye, which is how I always thought of my great friend Mozella. Meeting him brought further strength to my belief that nobody's perfect, and I know that more than anyone.

He carried around with him a signed photograph of the English theatre legend Sir Hubert Hearthwright. It was his sole possession, other than the sack, and I thought it rather sweet the way he clutched at it. He later told me he was a British soldier who had walked all the way here from France amidst the war. We all laughed and asked him how he had come so far without being shot—he just looked at us as if he didn't know. Whatever, we kept his identity secret. His real name was Felix Francis, but we called him Mozella from then on.

Nobody really cared who we were in there anyway: All crazy people were the same to them. It also didn't matter where we were from, because there was only one place we were going: Nowhere.

What did matter was that the three of us became great friends. None of us were much good at sleeping, and so we would lie awake in our little cots at night and listen to the bombs falling outside. Sometimes I would hear bombs that weren't there, and sometimes Mugle would hear them, and sometimes Mozella would hear his own explosions. "Did you hear that one?" became a catchphrase of ours those nights.

"No, not that one," we'd often reply.

"But do you hear that one?" I thought I'd hear a big bomb go off.

"No," they'd reply: "I can't hear anything above that booming noise!"

We were good friends. We told each other things we had never told anybody before. Vincent Mugle told us he had always been a starving artist, crawling the streets of France, drawing on anything. He had even drawn on the humps of crippled sailors, and been rewarded for his works. I admired his honesty, which inspired me to tell them the first true version of my life before coming to the asylum.

Previously, if anyone ever asked, I always told them that I had been raised by armadillos. But this was only partly true. Thanks to my new friends, I felt I could be myself for the very first time. But who was myself?

FOURTEEN

The life of Max Spurning "before the asylum". In his own words.

I was born Maximilian Schpurnstein in the small town of Lorrenstein, Germany, 1882. I lived with a large family, who were somewhat hostile. We were very poor and I felt very useless. I ran away from home in my early teens, fleeing to the larger city of Blasko to seek my fortune. I wanted to be an artist or an actor like the friends I later met. I wanted to entertain; to bring happiness to those who were unhappy like me.

I joined the circus to fulfil my dreams, falling under the charms of a fat clown named Waldo. He was a sweaty fellow, who smelled of cheese. At first, he employed me to look after the animals, although they didn't like me (especially the armadillos). My only friends were the little people, which is why I later cast them in my films. I even made a movie star of the bearded lady, whom I never really liked: She would swallow raw eggs and undress me with her eyes. I also wasn't crazy about her unkempt beard. But I never forgot these special people.

It wasn't long before Waldo grew tired of seeing me hanging around, and, as he couldn't feed me to the armadillos, thought I would serve better as a performer. So, at the age of sixteen, I first stepped onstage as "Electro-Boy". For the audiences' fun, Waldo pumped volts of electricity into my backside. The constant shocks animated me into a strange little dance, like a string-less puppet. And this, the audience found funny, though sometimes, today, I still twitch. As my career has proven, however, I soon learnt not to question the entertainment value of such an act. I could withstand the electric shocks, and thus, withstand anything. But, because I almost died night after night, this eventually had to stop. The electricity did, however, jolt my facial hair into premature bloom; for that I am eternally thankful: You may not know it, but there is always something that can be mistaken for light in every dark spot of life. I often think of my life as one big dark spot.

My next job as "Chicken Boy" was less successful. I thought I looked rather handsome in my suit, my moustache protruding through the feathers. The audience thought I resembled something ridiculous and booed me from the stage, hurling rotten fruit. I left, weeping: Waldo had sold me as a human-sized chicken; I had only sold myself as a human chicken-sized failure.

My happiest times were as the "Human Toadstool". The little people would perch upon my head, dressed as pixies, chirping and gibbering for the crowd's delight. This had to stop when Waldo saw we were having too much of a good time with this act. To this day, my head is slightly flat.

Then came "Rat Boy". Buried underground, I was forced to tunnel my way out and frighten the unwary audience standing above. I couldn't see a thing in that hideous rat outfit (my moustache protruding through the fur), so I could never find my way out of the ground on cue. Indeed, I often emerged to an empty crowd. As punishment, Waldo made the bearded lady sit on me. Since then, I have always equated animal costumes with failure. I have never worn one since.

The humiliation of those times drove me to drink. As a result, I can't remember the remainder of my past before I ended up in the hospital. Perhaps there were more animal costumes, perhaps more failure? I just remember waking one day, feeling sorry for myself in unfamiliar surroundings; my hangover seemed as nothing, though, when I learned I was in an asylum. Dark, alone, frightened and hungry—what I needed was hard liquor. What I got were my friends. One day we hatched a plan to escape.

FIFTEEN

Spurning's disembodied voice crackles from the spools . . .

[. . .] two bottles of gin and I'm anybody's . . . [*indecipherable noises*] . . . never work with armadillos . . . the Clay Men were loathsome figures. We fashioned them from the lumps of clay given to us by the orderlies, for use in our art. The fact that we wanted to do something in the asylum other than scream and babble obviously amused them.

We called the stuff they gave us clay, but it was barely pliable, dough-like dirt, swept up off the floor. Bristles of glass stuck out from it, cutting our hands. Our fellow inmates seemed wary of us as we sculpted, which made us feel bad, but they were also frightened of invisible insects and certain cheeses, so, as ever, we couldn't win. If an orderly passed by, we would hide the clay pieces beneath our cots and smile and act like we weren't making Clay Men. It's hard to believe they never cottoned on. And it's hard to act like you're not making Clay Men when you are.

Finally, after nights of hard toil and stealth, we had assembled the shapeless, lumbering figures: Life-size monsters, the Clay Men would help us escape. We were always seeking a way out. For our last days in the hospital, we would lie in our little cots at night and discuss ideas. Our first plan, suggested by Mugle, had been to dress as roosters and cluck our way free; after all, no one would notice three men in rooster suits. But I couldn't go through with it. As the idea involved animal costumes, it made me go funny round the eyes. Thankfully, you can't find a rooster suit in an asylum anywhere.

Then Mugle suggested we dig our way out with a shard of glass. I told him this plan was impossible also, whilst growing pale at memories of "Rat Boy". Thank God we each lacked the strength to cut through sheer stone with glass.

Then Mugle suggested that we crawl up a stray moonbeam spilling in through our window. "We shall escape into the sky!" he declared.

"Don't be ridiculous," I boomed, my moustache quivering: "How would we fit through the bars?" Thank God we couldn't fit through the bars (sometimes we didn't think straight, but, being incarcerated, we could be excused).

I'm proud to say that the Clay Men were my idea. One stormy night, appropriate for our caper, we put them into action. Mugle, Mozella and I each took a Clay Man and snuck our way through the long, twisting corridors to the main door, which was always heavily guarded and locked. If anyone got in our way (and they did), we hid behind our Clay Men and went: *Raaarrghh*. And our opponents went: *Aaaaarrrgghh*—and collapsed a little against the walls.

Scurrying past Herr Hoffmann's office (we could hear him in there, eating sausages), we finally reached the main door and *raaarrghhed* at the guard on duty: "We are Clay Men! Let us out!" We even swung our little clay fists at him—but only softly, not enough to bruise. The frightened guard duly complied and unbolted the door; he didn't want the Clay Men in his asylum—and he stepped through his own urine to prove it.

Once free, we danced about the gardens with our helpful friends of clay.

"That was fun," I said to my comrades: "We should do it more often."

It wasn't something we could do every day, granted. But, armed with our Clay Men, we took off through the empty streets for the first time in over a year.

The war was over, yet we still walked in its shadow. But we walked as free men; anything that imprisoned us after the war was only brought on by ourselves—or so we were led to believe.

The Clay Men proved to be our first experiment with fear; something the three of us would become masters of over the coming years. Slouching on the riverbanks that grey yet fateful day, Mozella concocted something about the Clay Men coming to life. "Wouldn't it be funny if they came to life?" I think were his exact words. We all laughed and agreed: "Yes, it would." Surprising as it may sound, from this small comment our futures were made . . .

Here the tape sputters to an end. Spurning would be silenced forever by a heart attack in June 1956.

SIXTEEN

Hollywood, 1967. Again.

Morbius Mozella is tired. He can't quite remember how he got home, but dimly recalls bring carried down Hollywood Boulevard by a tribe of dancing fools. Although he never participated in their disgusting revelry, he still feels somewhat "funny". It's an effect that people have on him.

Too weary to continue his memoirs, he puts on an old film instead; anything to keep the night at bay. The movie he chooses is one of his own; among the first he ever made. Although *Clay Men* (aka *Men of Clay* [1920]) is a seminal classic of fantastic cinema, it hasn't been shown in years. Right now, it's flickering across the old actor's wall: Three incarcerated lunatics (played by Mozella, Vincent Mugle and Max Spurning) attempt to escape. Their plan is simple: As the lunatics like to make unusual art with materials provided by the orderlies, they sculpt the Clay Men of the title. With a logic that could only come screaming from a madman's brain, they intend to "frighten" their way out of the asylum with these grotesque effigies. Mozella, however, is well-versed in Black Arts and, via a few misspelled captions, brings the creatures to life.

The monsters run amok, leaving a trail of murder and mayhem in their muddy midst. Strangling patients and orderlies alike, the three Clay Men are also portrayed (with frightening realism) by Mozella, Mugle and Spurning. Mozella remembers well, smearing each other in clay for the right effect (Spurning is only recognisable through the crude make-up as his moustache sticks out). He also recalls creating the acclaimed cardboard sets of jolting, unusual angles, designed to instil an appropriate terror. The three men aimed to make films that allowed glimpses of their distorted insides, hollowing out their imaginations onto the cheapest film stock they could steal.

Clay Men revolutionised the cinema. Shot with a single camera ("borrowed" from a nascent German film studio that was closed at the time), the film was all the more shocking upon initial release as the young filmmakers claimed it to be "Based on a true story"—a bold legend that remains a tribute to disbelief.

But there she is!

The Clay Men fall in love with one of the inmates, a vision known as Angel, played by Elizabeth, who remains oblivious to their lumped affections, blinded as she is by her own assumed madness. Nevertheless, the Clay Men tear each other apart, battling for her love.

The girl stares out blindly into the rising sun as it filters through barred windows. Clad in white shroud, like a dying ember, she stands alone on stony darkness, surrounded by misshapen lumps of clay. Torn shreds of shadow writhe upon the walls. The lunatics never do escape. *Fin.*

Mozella weeps on seeing his angel Elizabeth up there on the screen once more, so young and full of life. He turns to her in her casket, and cries out hard. Lifting his memoirs from the desk, he reads, through blurry eyes, of the times when they first met. These are the parts that have to be written perfectly; each word must stand testament to a love that shared a thousand dreams; all of which were awoken from, screaming.

SEVENTEEN

Mozella scans the empty page with roving, sorrowed orbs. His pen clutched tight between arachnid fingers, he takes a breath and writes:

Since I first beheld her . . .

"No." He scribbles over that first sight of her and starts again.

Since that first startling vision of her . . .

That doesn't sound right, either; it doesn't justify the moment: That first exact instant when these feelings were born.

When I first saw her, she seared my soul . . . my soul was seared . . . with sweet, black flames. . . sweeping over me . . . in one . . . agonizing . . .jolt . . . of heartbreak.

"One agonizing jolt of heartbreak?"

. . . my soul was seared with sweet, black flames, soaring over me in one sweeping itch . . .

. . . one agonizing itch . . .

. . . one agonizing jolt of heartbreak . . .

"No, no, no." He attacks the page once more.

I felt I had known her forever. She spoke to me and I died inside . . . My insides . . . dissolved . . . She was an

angel. She was divine.
>He reads it back.
>*Oh, damn it all to Hell!*
>There are no words.

EIGHTEEN

Holstenslava, Germany, 1919.

Thrashing winds, like the breath of Mephisto, tear through a gloom-soaked sky in which an ailing moon throws dim light upon a disarray of smoking rooftops, jutting towards the heavens from uneven cobbles. Upon these streets there scuttle three lunatics, freshly escaped. One is all bone with glowing eye; one is all hair with teeth; and one is all groomed moustache, with glowing eyes and teeth.

All three are dressed in shabby, borrowed overcoats several sizes too large, as they scamper through the wind and feathered snows, passing the dark, unmoving waters of an infested canal, where moon-glows lie in shatters, acting as spotlights for the plague-ridden theatrics of the local rats.

Buildings line the canal like crumbling hives, housing an intense flurry of people, hectic as insects, yet absent as ghosts. Outside, the madmen lope up alleys like shrieks through gullets, casting deranged shadows across the shuttered windows and cracked cold stone of this Godforsaken town. "Holstenslava" says the leaning signpost, bent beneath the storm.

The lunatics like this place: It suits their temperament.

From town to town, they have sought a home; finding shelter in abandoned huts, warmed only by their dreams. If a dilapidated barn cannot be found, then a bar is preferable, for obvious reasons, and it is one hovel in particular that persuades them to stay.

A cement stairway leads them down below the deserted street. Passing through heavy velvet curtains, they behold a small, low-ceilinged room with lighting just as low. Groups sit drinking at high, wobbling tables, on high wooden chairs, emitting thick smoke before a dimly lit stage.

At the centre of it all is Herr Archibald Grott, an ex-circus performer turned bar owner, who has named his unique establishment "Der Zauber-Schauer" ("The Magic Shower"; or is it "Magic Shudder"?). Grott can be found standing behind the bar, keeping owlish vigilance. Whenever anyone approaches for a drink, his watchfulness slips, and he pretends to busy himself in the cleaning of glasses. The serving is left to one exhausted young girl (possibly Grott's daughter, maybe his mistress?). Behind the overworked girl there sits an old woman (possibly Grott's mother, maybe his mistress?), who puffs on everlasting cigarettes, perfectly still.

Herr Grott is a man of wide interests, far happier immersed in the art of taxidermy than leaping through hoops or serving beer. Sometimes, with the encouragement of drink, he performs his old acts on his own stage (the only platform that will now allow him). His new act, however, is proudly displayed in the bar's garish decorations, stuffed as it is with bric-a-brac and ghoulish artefacts, running the gamut of the ex-clown's mordant tastes.

Protruding from the walls and pillars stare the blank faces of stuffed beasts, whose wiry, dead hair grazes the customers' arms as they step away from the bar. Dirty yellow skeletons hang from the walls on rusting chains; coffin lids greet those foolhardy enough to sit in a certain booth; and, strangest of all, one dark corner secludes a zebra with an emaciated goat smiling sadly on its back. Both animals are stuffed, though those other unfortunate animals—the clientele—are very much alive.

Der Zauber-Schauer is one big theatre, isolated from the mundane society that crawls unwittingly above. Passing across the stage, before a backdrop of tattered cloth bearing abstract shards of paint, are such varied entertainments as Hans Kranovitch and his wrestling dwarves; Stefan Lowenstein and his cardboard box; and Ernst Kublisch, an organist whose hands, having two thumbs and eight fingers on each, possess twice as many digits than nature usually allows. It is a divine mystery to see those many fingers race across the keys like fumbling spiders, churning out a cascade of discordant notes and eerie melody.

To the accompaniment of Herr Kublisch's multi-fingered compositions, Lilli Winkler performs her bewitching striptease. Pulling the last rag from her shapely, writhing form, she drinks in the halting applause of a befuddled audience, when she reveals herself to be of neither sex.

In this brave underworld, you are whoever you want to be; and as Fraulein Winkler identifies as a woman, then a woman she is. Though this doesn't stop whispers flying amongst the patrons: It is well known that Kublisch and Winkler enjoy a further relationship to their "musical" one.

But here, nonconformity is applauded, and individuality comes before gender, race and creed. No one is a stranger, but all are entitled to be strange: Women smoke cigars in top hats and monocles, and men don make-up and fancy dress. It doesn't matter who you are; as long as you don't harm others, acceptance is rife. And this is why the place is deemed unusual.

Justly fascinated, the lunatics return night after night. They have finally found somewhere warm in which they can sit, fuelling their wishes with intoxicating elixirs procured for them from the bar. Gentility and alcohol flows in a manner all three gentlemen are unaccustomed to, for, despite their problems, they are ingratiating chaps. No one even cares that Mozella is English. In fact, they don't know what he is, as he speaks in the same indecipherable dialect as his friends. Crawling the country together for so long has made it hard to distinguish where one lunatic ends and another begins; an intimacy first bred in the asylum they've escaped.

Meeting new faces is just what they need, so they acquaint themselves with every regular patron of Der Zauber-Schauer. From Hans Kranovitch, who introduces them to each of his wrestling dwarves, to Herr Kublisch, who grants them an introduction to every one of his surplus fingers.

Initially, Herr Grott also likes the lunatics (they remind him of himself when young), but he soon tires of finding them passed out beneath his tables, and offers them more legitimate lodgings upstairs.

The three itinerants find themselves sharing a small, room-like cubicle above the bar, packed with an array of stuffed and mounted creatures. In the corner of the room, the strange old woman rumoured to be Herr Grott's mother or lover, sits immobile on a ramshackle stool, watching them with squashed-currant eyes as they toss and turn on jaundiced sheets. Compared to the madhouse, it is luxury.

On expressing his appreciation of their unholy act, Mozella frequently finds himself the houseguest of Ernst Kublisch and Lilli Winkler. He finds that the rumoured live-in lovers are actual live-in lovers, who live-in conveniently nearby.

Kublisch owns a small apartment in a fashionable area of town, which not only houses his stripper girlfriend of unknown gender, but also many useless gadgets of his own invention. He keeps his sixteen fingers and four thumbs busy, that's for sure.

Kublisch has machines for everything he should be able to do himself, from preparing his breakfast to making his bed. All of his creations are rodent-generated. He figures the local rats are more useful powering his contraptions than chewing innocent ankles or spreading plague. He has them running happily in little wheels, generating more power than expected for pincer-fingered robots to churn out sausages and lightly boiled eggs.

It is music, however, that brings Mozella to the Kublisch residence. Keen to emulate the sounds of his idol, J.S. Bach, Mozella patiently learns the rudiments of the organ under Kublisch's instruction. It isn't long before Kublisch and Winkler invite the skull-faced young man to live with them, leaving Spurning and Mugle to their filthy sheets and vigilant pensioner. Mozella happily obliges. He sleeps below the organ, on rags; usually the frilled garments Lilli discards during her act.

In this pit of dark velvet hangings and mad contraptions, Mozella furthers his organ studies. He's a quick learner, attracting ideas and formations to his sticky mind. The curious couple enjoy that sticky mind, Lilli especially. When Ernst goes upstairs to fetch a record to listen to, or a scrap of music to study, she suddenly leaps up and urges Mozella to run away with her. Planting open-mouthed kisses on his once-untouched lips, she snuggles dangerously close. A stranger to relationships and hermaphrodites, Mozella grows even more pale, squirming from her affections through a façade of quiet ignorance. When Kublisch returns, Lilli slides to her original position by the organ, listening to Mozella play, with angels in her eyes but devils on the brain.

Sometimes, when he's alone with Herr Kublisch, Mozella feels the suspicious sensation of twenty fumbling digits creeping across his buttocks. This is ignored as best as it can be. Mozella forgives his hosts' human urges for their inhuman kindnesses.

Unlike his hosts, Mozella's passion is confined to music, a subject they discuss long into the night. They also talk about literature, art, and the latest sensation: Das Kinema, which they liken to an animated dream. Theatrical conversation allows Mozella to impart the embellished truths of his own fledgling life as an actor, a life he longs to return to. Such interests embolden the trio, and Kublisch and Winkler eventually introduce their tenant to a friend, and fellow patron of Der Zauber-Schauer, the theatre manager, Rotwang Schule.

Schule is a stern man with a fair wealth of knowledge and anecdotes he is reluctant to repeat. He runs workshops below his little theatre for unseasoned actors, and thus, Mozella is invited to attend. Although he feels an inexorable need to express himself through such arts, Mozella is blighted and beset by crippling nerves.

Under Schule's tuition, however, he learns a lot, mutating himself from a bedraggled interpreter of words, to a man who knows his own soul; whether postulating on the emotions and character of vegetables, or simply endearing himself to new strangers with shared interests: No small feat in itself. The most valuable lesson he learns here, however, is that you will get nowhere in the acting profession unless you are prepared to look like an idiot. And under the guidance of Rotwang Schule, Mozella looks like an idiot quite happily for two nights of every week.

He also has trouble sleeping, a problem that has gnawed at him since birth. Most times, despite his newfound complacency, he simply can't—it seems the hardest thing in the world, to simply relax and switch himself off. Others accomplish this with appropriate ease, so why should he find it such a burden?

When the Angel of Sleep *does* visit Mozella's bed of rags, strange things happen. On more than one occasion, Morbius has risen in sleep to hover by Kublisch's bed. Through the delusions of his sleepwalk, Mozella admires the organist's bone-white ankles peeping from the tangled sheets and mistakes them for ham hocks. Kublisch always wakes with a yowl when Mozella's teeth sink into his calves. They laugh about it later, of course. But they find little to laugh about when Mozella takes his nocturnal habits outside, meandering the streets, prowling by windows and lurking by doors, as lonely a night-stroller as any sewer rat.

On finding him gone, Kublisch and Winkler run out in their nightclothes, usually discovering their sleepwalking lodger collapsed in the rain.

When Mozella is sighted sleepwalking through undesirable establishments he would usually be loath to frequent, reports pile in around Der Zauber-Schauer, amidst great mirth, that Mozella has an evil doppelganger. How shocked they are, they gasp through their smiles, to see Mozella's unmistakable form standing silently in a disreputable bar, savouring each lurid sight with drowsing eyeballs. How they laugh at their dark horse friend.

Mozella's uniqueness is also his problem: With his livid eyes and skull-like head, he simply cannot be mistaken for anyone else. Even when he's sleeping, he walks in a unique, half-hunched, half-upright, tiptoe stride, his skeletal body dwarfed within the big black overcoat from which his long bony fingers protrude. The back of his head is lightly cracked—the only reminder of a father he never speaks of. It is from this lightly cracked head that his dreams and fears burst forth.

Although he rarely sleeps, he lives in a perpetual nightmare. He fears that, should he remain inactive, his brain will rot in its cage of bone, so he spends every spare hour composing at Kublisch's organ, sculpting sounds from the silence, forsaking food and rest. By the light of a solitary candle, he structures lyrics around his haunted noise. (Two albums of Mozella's music, *The Many Moods of Morbius Mozella* and *15 Bygones*, recorded during his time in Germany, were released to cash-in on the actor's ill-fated comeback in 1967. As no one bought them then, both records are now collector's items.)

Kublisch is impressed by Mozella's music, feeling, deep down, that he has taught his student little: Whatever skill Mozella possesses comes from some almighty fire burning within. The flames continue to roar, but now is the time for them to spread out from his guts, and into the world outside.

NINETEEN

Der Zauber-Schauer, Holstenslava, 1919.

The audience descends into Herr Grott's establishment, hoping to chase the hard-toiling day from their minds. A spotlit Ernst Kublisch takes to the stage, wringing his multi-fingered hands:

"Good evening. Ahem. We only see the world through our own eyes. No one else can see it through them. In fact, I have no way of proving that what I see is what you see. And it is through these individual views that we make up our world. Thus, every one of us is important; every one of us is unique. And here to bring his own little world to yours . . . May I present: Morbius Mozella—the Man with No Eyes in His Face!"

A light smattering of applause.

Kublisch races to his organ at the side of the stage and emits a low, faint hum from the keys. Morbius Mozella steps into the light, a jangling shadow; his eyes smeared beneath black make-up. The audience falls silent at the figure's unusual appearance;

they've never been so entranced by stillness. As the organ noise rises, the shadow suddenly speaks, raising an arm in weary gesture, his voice a tender moan:

"I am the man with no eyes in his face!

"Now, how could it be that this is the case?

"Well, let me tell you how it came to be; that I lost both my eyes, yet still I could see!

"It all began one sad day in June; I levered my left eye right out with a spoon.

"The reasons for doing so might not seem so clear, but it was all for a girl whom I held so dear.

"Her name was Jane, how I longed for her grace; but she longed for another, as was often the case.

"So, in fits of self-loathing, I savaged my face—and tore my left eyeball right out of place.

"A man with one orb could never be her lover, so I picked up my spoon and poked out the other.

"As you might guess, I was quite upset; and justifiably steeped in regret.

"Yet, I had only myself to blame—after all, I gouged my eyes out—not Jane.

"But she was the reason behind my insanity; and hers is the name that is now a profanity; as I speak it with anger, sadness and fear—how is pain consummated when you can't shed a tear?

"I was quite scared; in fact, I was frightened. Through magnified emotions, my senses were heightened!

"Shoulders shrugged high, with hands deep in pockets, I now view the world through empty black sockets; gaping and lonely for the company of orbs, lonely for love and all it absorbs.

"Cobwebs settle where my eyes used to be, so I brush away the spiders, and set the flies free."

"My confidence is gone and trashed, now the windows to my soul are smashed!

"All those who saw me knew not where to look; some of them shivered, most of them shook.

"And through lack of vision, I saw every face; I felt every feeling of leaving this place.

"So, I turned from my friends and I ran and I ran; into the streets as fast as I can!

"And the rain fell so heavy from a sky that was dull, as it entered my sockets and filled up my skull; and ran down my face, just like false tears; yet never before had I cried so sincere.

"It was then that I realised: Although I'm in pain, those who have nothing, have something to gain."

Silence. The audience don't know what to make of this. Suddenly, the doors slam open and there's a shriek from the back:

"Polizei!"

Four burly policemen push their way through the crowd. Striding onstage, they drag Mozella down and tear Kublisch from his organ. Now the audience applauds. Once the performers have been bundled away, a deathly hush falls over the place, broken here and there by grave whispers. Hans Kranovitch and his wrestling dwarves take to the stage, and the audience soon forgets.

TWENTY

Holstenslava Police Station, 1919.

Mozella sits quivering in a grotto-like cell beneath the station. The Inspector stands over him, monocled and stiff.

"Why are you so nervous?"

Mozella is always nervous. He shrinks inside his large black coat, damp eyes rolling for a faraway place. Why does he have to stumble into trouble all the time? All he wants is to be left alone. People always have to poke their noses in and make him feel wrong. Right now, the Inspector is the one with the poky nose.

"Do you know why you're here?"

Mozella shakes his head. He guesses he's here on a charge of obscenity due to his act. It's not unusual for such charges to be brought forth against the performers and patrons of Der Zauber-Schauer.

The Inspector peers at Mozella as if he were a slug on his new, polished boot.

"A girl is dead. Murdered. At least, we think it's

a girl. We believe you may know her. Lilli Winkler?"

Mozella gasps.

"You do know her?"

"Yes. Yes, I live with her. She's . . . murdered?"

"It has been said that you have a violent temper."

Mozella can only respond with a nervous wheeze.

"You have attacked people in the night," the Inspector continues.

"Yes, but only in my sleep."

"Only in your sleep?"

"Yes, I sleepwalk."

"Sleepwalk?"

"Yes. Or I used to. I don't anymore."

"Why not?"

"Because I no longer sleep."

"You no longer sleep?"

"No."

"Then what do you do when you ought to be sleeping?"

"When I ought to have been sleeping, and was sleeping, I was walking; when I ought to have been sleeping, and haven't been sleeping, I've not been sleeping. Or playing my organ, usually."

"What?"

"I don't sleep anymore."

"No?"

"No."

"Then what do you do with your nights?"

"I write. I play my organ."

"You write music?"

"Yes. And poetry, and stories."

"Do you ever write about . . . murder?"

"Sometimes."

"I would like to read these stories."

"I'm not sure if they're fit for public view."

"Oh? Why not?"

"I don't think they're ready."

"What kind of murders do you write about? The murders of young girls—of strippers of unknown sex?"

"No," Mozella stammers. "I write what the story dictates."

The Inspector's face crumples. "The story *dictates*?"

"Yes."

"And what do these stories *dictate*?"

"Well, when you're writing, the characters just take over."

"Oh, really. And who are these characters? Are they your friends?"

"I wouldn't say that."

"Then what *would* you say?"

"Sorry?"

"Mr Mozella, where were you on the evening of April 23rd?"

"Is that today?"

The Inspector nods, then looks at his watch. "Yesterday," he corrects.

"I was pacing the backstage area of Der Zauber-Schauer. Waiting to perform."

"And what were you going to perform? Murder? One of the murders in your stories—the ones that your friends *dictate* to you?"

"No. I was going to perform my poem "The Man with No Eyes in His Face". My friend, Ernst Kublisch, accompanied me on organ. You saw the performance yourself; at least, you interrupted it."

The Inspector brushes away Mozella's comments like flies around a sandwich. "And who is this man with no eyes in his face? Another friend of yours?"

"I am the man with no eyes in his face."

"But I see eyes in your face. Two of them, in fact. They're looking at me right now. They're slightly damp."

"Yes. It's just a character."

"Oh, these characters again. Tell me more about these characters."

"I don't know where to start."

"You can start by telling me more about your relationship with Herr Ernst Kublisch."

"Ernst is my friend. My mentor. We have lived together for a couple of months now."

"And who else lives with you?"

"Fraulein Winkler. My other friend."

"She is dead," the Inspector drones. "Tell me, what was the relationship between Kublisch and Winkler?"

"They performed together."

"In what way?"

"In every way."

There's a clang as the Inspector's monocle drops to the floor. Suddenly a little man in uniform enters the cage. "It's all right, Inspector," he says. "You can let him go."

"Why?" The Inspector looks furious. "Has the other one admitted to it?"

The little man shakes his head. "There's no need. The gentleman next door has a total of sixteen fingers and four thumbs."

"So?"

"Well, sir, that would explain the four thumb prints and sixteen finger marks we found on the victim's throat."

"Yes, I suppose it would." The Inspector turns to Mozella: "You can go. But I'll be keeping my eye on you."

Mozella gets up and leaves, feeling none the wiser and twice as alone.

.

TWENTY-ONE

If the town of Holstenslava was strange to Mozella before, it's even stranger now: His home is no longer a home; it's a murder site. He's confused to say the least.

In this gloomy state of confusion, the last two people he needs to see are his friends, Vincent Mugle and Max Spurning, but that's exactly who he goes to see. As usual, they are sitting in squalor at their small apartment above Der Zauber-Schauer. The silent old lady watches them, and they watch her back.

"Mozella!" they chime as he steps through their door.

Spurning rises to greet him, helping his friend wade through the clutter. ("The Clutter" is largely made up of Mugle's discarded paintings of the spiritually deformed.)

"Great show last night," says Spurning, unconvincingly: "We really enjoyed it."

Mugle cuts straight to the point. "What were the police doing there?"

Mozella explains. The others look as if they're trying to understand.

"It just goes to show," says Spurning.

"You never really know anyone," Mugle concludes.

"Ouch!" Mozella hits his head on the ceiling. The room is so small that Mugle's beard tickles everyone present. The old lady sneezes.

Mozella points at her. "Can she hear us?"

Spurning shakes his moustache. "She has no ears."

"Really?" Mozella spies the glass on the bedside cabinet containing her false ears. "Do they actually work?"

"I've never seen her wear them," says Mugle, "but they worked when we put them on."

"Did they work when you took them off?"

"Yes, they did, as a matter of fact."

"You fools," Mozella spurts. "You both have perfectly good ears, and that's what you were hearing with, whether you wore an old crone's false ones or not."

"Oh, yes," says Mugle. "We knew that."

Spurning glares at Mozella's head. "Where are *your* ears?"

"Never mind my ears," says Mozella, weary of

the topic, "I have no home."

"You can stay here with us," says Mugle. "If you can find a space."

Looking at "The Clutter", this seems unlikely. "It will be just like the good old days," the artist smiles.

"What?" says Mozella. "When we were locked up in an asylum?"

"Ja," says Spurning, dipping his hand into "The Clutter". He pulls up a clunky machine.

"What's that?" asks Mozella.

"It's a Kamera," Spurning grins. "I am filming you now."

"Where did you get it from?" Mozella shields himself from its whirring glare. "We don't have any money."

Mugle laughs. "We took it from a film studio in Berlin."

You stole it?"

"Ja," says Spurning. "Oh, don't look so high and mighty. Haven't you just spent the last few hours in a police cell?"

"But I'm innocent," Mozella blurts.

"A likely story," Spurning sniffs.

"Anyway," Mugle jumps in: "We didn't steal the camera. We *borrowed* it."

"Ja, that's what I meant to say," says Spurning.

"We filmed your show last night, Morbius."

Mozella ignores him. "How did you steal this thing?"

"The Clay Men helped us," Mugle laughs.

Mozella suddenly notices one of the loathsome clay fellows poking up through "The Clutter". As well as bringing back bad memories, it adds further wonder to the small room's capacity.

"I'm going for a walk," he sighs.

TWENTY-TWO

Mozella did a lot of walking over the next few days. As he walked, he thought about life. Although not a religious man, per se, he did believe in the human soul and its longevity after death. He also believed in God; not as a bearded old man in the sky, but as a force; something that was all around, that could be tapped into at any time. Like electricity. Or an ocean, that we are all mere drops within.

Mozella couldn't help but feel that a higher force had made him miserable for a reason. Although he believed in choice, he also felt guided. *Maybe certain roads have to be travelled in order to reach my destiny?* He hoped the answers would become clear in the next life. He'd be sorely disappointed if they weren't.

He truly believed that life went on. It had to. Where did it all go otherwise? All the magic, all the feeling, the dreams, the ideals that whooshed within him like giant waves: How could they possibly be silenced? How could there ever be nothing? How could *we* ever be nothing? What *is* nothing?

There had just been a war, of course, and these seemed like godless times, yet Mozella still felt strangely spiritual. The popular argument amongst his existential friends, in light of the carnage they'd all been through, was how could a god let this happen? Mozella always responded, "But wasn't the war started by men?" Not God; just men with little willies and problems of their own.

Why didn't God come down and stop the bloody war? Why didn't He, in His power and wisdom, make things all better?

Although often unsure at the best of times, Mozella saw no sense in that. Why create life just to control it? Nothing could be learnt from that, so what was the point? Should God treat us like toy soldiers, picking us up each time we fall? Should He come down, and not only stop the wars He was blamed for starting, but also help us find lost socks and erase the smell of noxious farts? Should He come down and clean our houses, making us endless cups of tea, while we sit and vegetate?

Life wasn't supposed to be happy, or so Mozella believed. He felt it as a strange adventure, designed to take you somewhere else. Perhaps a higher plane? Or maybe just a hole in the ground, full of worms?

It was a test of some sort. It had to be: A horrible,

cruel rite that we all must endure. Mozella couldn't think of any other explanation. But then, he didn't know the answers any more than anyone else who pretended they did. *Always best to keep an open mind*, he mused; no matter what jumps in.

Like a wailing infant that won't be put to bed, Mozella's mind yammered on. He wasn't being melodramatic, but he couldn't stand life. It was hard to explain. He wanted to enjoy life, but he always felt like a broken doll, lost within the darkness of his gnarled insides. It was hard to see through the tangled, haunted forest ripping through his guts; it was hard not to sink in the gloom.

He lived for his creative pursuits, hanging onto them like driftwood amidst the torrents. And as much as he never felt a part of anything around him, he still had, at least, his private world. Was it preferable to the world outside where everyone else seemed to belong? People were, after all, only people; full of spit and sweat, and living, for all their forced ideals, to ram another meal in their stomachs. Some could afford to consume more food; others couldn't eat at all. But people were still only people; blind to any mystery within.

Mozella wore his heart very much on his sleeve. When he wasn't at a loss for a response, his answers were always honest, no matter how stupid they sounded. He ended each day wishing he'd said this, wishing he'd done that; wishing he'd done this or said that to a certain someone, the girl of his dreams. Everything he couldn't tell her, because she wasn't there, he'd impart to blank sheets. He felt like he had to, like he'd drown in the air if he couldn't.

He imagined love would make him happy, because nothing else had. But once he'd found love, he knew he would disappear in that feeling, devoting himself solely to his suitor, ensuring he never stirred from the dream of her. Contentment would come from living through another, as it did in the prison of his performances. But, as it happened, no love was forthcoming, and all he had were dreams that felt hopeless because they weren't shared. *You have to be pig-ignorant to be truly happy*, he thought. Unfortunately, or fortunately, he would never be that.

He looked at the points of his life thus far: If he had never been a soldier, he would never have been thrown into the asylum. If not for that, he would never have made clay men with Vincent and Max. Without them, he would never have found Holstenslava and characters like Ernst Kublisch. Without whom, Mozella would never have learnt to express himself creatively. Without that, life would have no meaning.

And if Ernst Kublisch had never throttled his lover, Mozella wouldn't be traipsing and thinking lost thoughts. He wouldn't feel the urge to step into an unfamiliar road, hoping a tram would knock him down. He wouldn't look up and see an angel: A tall, raven-haired beauty, who was helping a hedgehog across the road. Piano chords crashed through his head at the sight of her. He didn't know it then, but this radiant vision was Elizabeth, who would later become his wife and share his dreams. Hedgehog-walking was the first instance he would witness of her caring nature. Like Mozella, the prickle-backed creature had crawled out into the road, hoping to be squashed. But, as Elizabeth selflessly guided the poor animal to the other side, Mozella was enraptured: *If that girl looked at me the way she looks at that suicidal hedgehog, I will have found my way home.*

TWENTY-THREE

Although the "Hedgehog Lady" was a stranger, Mozella felt he'd known her all his life. Looking into her face, he saw her as a child, all elbows and knees in the sun and grass; as an elderly lady spinning yarns to doting children on firelit nights; and as she was then: A vision that grasped his heart and rendered him dumb.

As for the "Hedgehog Lady", she had yet to even acknowledge the one who stood adoring her. And before he knew it, she was gone.

Ensuring that the hedgehog was safe, she turned the corner, leaving nothing but a memory; a ghost to haunt his thoughts. But through the tingling sadness, he felt weirdly uplifted—as if certain he would see her again.

And he did. Eventually.

But, back then, all he could do was stand staring at the empty space she'd once filled, as frozen as a gorgon's victim (yet this was the loveliest Medusa ever to turn the flesh of man into stone).

Over the next few weeks, Mozella returned to

Eckhorn Road (the name of the spot), hoping she'd return. For twenty-one nights, he stood on the street corner, like a forlorn statue, in wind, rain and snow. To those who witnessed his lovesick stance, Mozella became something of a local legend. Old Holstenslavers still remember the goblin of their childhood days, the one they called "He Who Waits for the Hedgehog Lady". They recall with gurgling fondness how they would dance up and down to torment him; or try to make him smile and move (which he never did). They'd hang baubles from his bony protrusions and stuff dead flowers down his trousers. Hedgehogs nestled at his feet. *She'll have to come and walk these things soon*, he thought.

Vincent and Max came down often. "Stop making a fool of yourself," they'd beg. But Mozella wouldn't listen. He was a man in love. In fact, he had always behaved like a man enraptured: He never slept, he rarely ate, he was sick in the head and heart . .Then, on the twenty-first night of his vigil, she came back, a school of scuttling hedgehogs at her feet. Oh, how lovely were her feet! And all the rest of her, too.

She is finally here, Mozella thought. *But what the hell am I supposed to do now?*

What should I say? What should I do?

Perhaps I should say hello? And then . . . offer to help her walk the hedgehogs? Compliment her on her hedgehogs?

No, I'll . . .

He remained as still and silent as he had for the last twenty-one days. Once the hedgehogs were escorted to safety, she passed him by yet again.

Despondent as ever, Mozella stood frozen through the night. On the twenty-second morning, he had an idea. Jolting into life, he walked, a little stiffly, on weak, malnourished legs, to Vincent and Max's apartment.

"Why do you want our rug?" they clamoured, as Mozella slid the old lady off it. Tucking the dusty carpet in a roll beneath his arm, he marched out, saying nothing. He was a desperate man.

On the way back to Eckhorn Road, he collected fallen branches. Piercing the twigs through the old brown rug, he draped it over his shoulders and crawled out into the middle of the road.

Disguising himself as a hedgehog, it seemed, was the only way he could get her to notice him. If she would guide him across the road and lavish, just for one moment, the same level of care and affection upon himself as she did to those prickly little beasts, then his life would be complete.

He curled up and waited. After three buses and two zimmer frames had rolled across his back, he was tempted to call it a night. But then she came again.

"I assume you are 'He Who Waits for the Hedgehog Lady'," her silken voice purred.

Mozella huddled beneath his twiggy rug. *If people call me that, then word has obviously got around. What a romantic, noble title.*

"I do not like being referred to as a 'hedgehog lady'," came the voice from above. "My name is Elizabeth."

Mozella looked up, dazzled by beauty. "Elizabeth," he stammered. "I am . . ."

"You are a fool."

Mozella lowered his head.

"Besides," she continued, "I already have a suitor."

Glancing up, Mozella saw a young man skulking behind her. He would recognise that twirly moustache anywhere.

Max Spurning! My best friend! How could he?

But Max gave only a faintly apologetic look as he led Elizabeth away.

Sinking beneath his doleful disguise, Mozella wanted to die. Yet, despite the sadness of the scene, a lesson had been learnt: Until you have crawled at the feet of the woman you love in a hedgehog costume, only to be spurned because she is in the arms of your so-called best friend, then you have never known humiliation.

This incident would inspire the premise of *Hedgehog Man* (1954)—Mozella's last film before his '67 comeback (which he made as a form of therapy following Elizabeth's death). I wish I could say that, with this picture, some good had come from a painful episode, but the movie was terrible. Mozella would never dress as a hedgehog again.

TWENTY-FOUR

Mozella sat on the riverbank, staring into brown waters. He wondered what a woman like Elizabeth could see in a man like Max (his supposed friend). Then he saw his skull-headed reflection glaring back at him. *No wonder she couldn't love me*, he thought. *I have no facial hair.*

Max, on the other hand, had a fine moustache. Perhaps its bristly nature reminded Elizabeth of her beloved hedgehogs?

But, if that was so, then the sight of Mozella in a damn good, if rudimentary, hedgehog costume should have incited similar affection?

Mozella needed answers. With none forthcoming from a river full of rain, he decided to go and rap sadly on Max's door. His former friend answered, looking as dishevelled as his room.

"Come in, Morbius."

Mozella entered and sat on the old lady's knee. He wished he'd thought of doing this on previous visits, as he found her withered thighs more comforting than the floor.

Looking around, trying to avoid Max's gaze, he noticed that Mugle wasn't there. *He must be out somewhere.*

"Where's Mugle?"

"He's out somewhere," Spurning replied.

"I thought so . . . How's Elizabeth?"

"She's fine."

"Dammit, Max. You knew I was waiting for her."

"I didn't."

"Yes, you did. Why else would the locals call me 'He Who Waits for the Hedgehog Lady'?"

"That was *you*?"

"You knew damn well it was."

Silence.

"But *how*?" Mozella suddenly exploded. "How did you do it? Is it your moustache? I wait, for days and nights on end . . . and you just win her heart so easily . . ."

"Well," Spurning blustered. "I just went over, said 'Hello. Do you like my moustache? Would you like to go to dinner?' And she said yes. To both my questions."

"You make it sound simple."

"It is. You just have to believe in yourself."

"How can I believe in myself when no one believes in me?"

"I believe in you."

"You believe in me enough to steal the girl that I love."

"It's not that. I just didn't approve of your methods."

Mozella didn't either, as it happened. He couldn't think of anyone else who would stoop to wearing that hedgehog costume. Not out of all the cranks he knew.

"I mean, you don't really know Elizabeth, do you?" said Spurning. "So, how can you love her? You just saw her walking a hedgehog across the road. And that seemed to be all it took."

Yes. It did seem to be all it took. But what Mozella felt was real. He was sure of it.

Tired of awkward confrontations, Max patted his friend on the arm. "Oh, well, better luck next time. Plenty of fish in the sea."

There were plenty of fish, but only one Elizabeth.

Mozella rose to leave. On reaching the door, he turned. "Do you love her, Max?"

Spurning cleared his throat. "Well, I wouldn't go that far." Then he gave a vulgar wink and shut the door.

Mozella stood awhile, screaming inside. Then the door swung open again and Max poked his head round with a look of regret: "Morbius?"

"Yes?"

"Can we have our rug back?"

TWENTY-FIVE

Mozella decided to take his own life. What was the point? Nobody loved him, nobody ever would. What was the sense in living a life that was merely endurance? He yearned for oblivion and rest.

Returning to the river, he stood glaring at the rushing tides into which he longed to dissolve. Then he caught his reflection. *I'm so ugly. No one could love me.* Bending down, he tore at his mirrored face with angry hands. Then, with a cry, he threw himself in.

Expecting to vanish below the dirty waters, he landed feet-first on a shallow riverbed. Agonizing pain shot up his legs, as the water swirled about his knees. A fish with big teeth snapped at his ankles. Yelling and splashing from his would-be grave, Mozella flopped, safe, on the riverbank, panting and wheezing. *A river too shallow to drown in. Humiliated by a fish.* His thoughts returned to death.

Walking along the road, his sodden shoes slapped the tarmac, until he saw an oncoming car. Leaping into its path, his head smashed the windscreen and dinted the bodywork. Screeching to a halt, a little man in round glasses hobbled out: "What do you think you are doing?"

Mozella was plastered across the bonnet, clinging to it as he used to his dreams. "I wish I was dead," he groaned.

"That can be arranged," said the driver, pulling out a pistol from his overcoat and aiming it at Mozella's head.

"Please get it over with," said Mozella.

Before the trigger could be pulled, a cry came from behind: *"Halt! Polizei!"* The little man was seized by two policemen. "We don't like little men who point guns at people's heads," one of them said as they dragged him away.

"I'll kill you for this, you skull-faced bastard," the angry motorist cried as he was carried, kicking and screaming, to the nearest police station.

As Mozella peeled himself off the man's car, he shuddered. *Who wants to live in a world full of maniacs like that?* His thoughts turned to death once more.

He made his way to Vincent and Max's residence. Vincent answered the door; Max was out with Elizabeth, which only furthered Mozella's suicidal leanings.

"Good to see you, Morbius," said Vincent.

Mozella cut straight to the point: "Do you still

have that hook in the ceiling on which you unsuccessfully tried to hang yourself last week?"

"Yes, why?"

Before Vincent could receive an answer, Mozella flung one of his shoelaces over the hook and tied it round his neck. Lifting his feet, he dangled from the ceiling. The old lady in the corner smiled as Vincent tried to stop him. "No, no! It will not take your weight!"

As if on cue, the hook ripped from the ceiling in a shower of plaster chunks and Mozella crashed down, ripping through a pile of Vincent's canvases.

"You fool! You have destroyed my work!"

Lurching up from the floor, Mozella simply grabbed a nearby palette knife and jabbed it into his chest. But the tool was too blunt and encrusted with paint to make any impression.

"Put the knife down, Morbius," said Vincent.

Mozella continued to hack away at his ribs. "No. I'm doing good. Look, blood!" He pointed to some red flecks on his shirt.

Vincent shook his head. "That is just paint, from the knife. Give it up now, Morbius."

Disappointed to discover that he wasn't spurting blood, Mozella put the blade down. Then Max entered: "Ah, Mozella! What a pleasant surprise."

Mozella bashed his head against the wall.

"We like your idea," Max enthused.

"This one?" said Mozella, nutting the wall.

"No."

Mozella clasped his head. There must be a less painful way to die. Spying a Clay Man in the corner, he ran over and tried to strangle himself in its arms.

"That's the idea we like," said Max. Vincent nodded at his side.

"What idea?" Mozella looked for a more practical way to do himself in.

"Clay Men," said Max, producing a stack of typewritten pages. "Your script. Vincent and I would like to film it with you."

Mozella stopped trying to drown himself in the thick flow of dribble that ran off the old lady's chin.

"Why not?" he smiled. "It might be fun."

TWENTY-SIX

Clay Men was not the first filmed experiment Mozella took part in. It was just the first one he was aware of. Spurning's previous directorial efforts, with Mugle offering assistance, had begun with *Mozella Beetle* (1919). In this self-explanatory short, Morbius Mozella turns into a beetle, a hearse, and the silent old lady who occupied the Spurning/Mugle apartment.

One hungover Sunday, with nothing better to do, they had secretly filmed Mozella looking nervous and mournful. Then, using the magic effect known as "stopping the camera and filming something else", Mozella suddenly turns into a beetle, a hearse, and the old woman. After he's done that, the word *Fin* appears, indicating, thankfully, that the movie is over.

Spurning and Mugle were so proud of their first effort that they collaborated on a second short that very same year. Again, they used Mozella as their subject. Not because he was particularly photogenic, but because he looked interesting. This next film,

Somnambulist, was a photographic record of one of Mozella's sleepwalks. In the movie, the sleeping Mozella can be seen frequenting bars, dancing with tramps, and falling into puddles, before he finally collapses in the street. Although both Spurning and Mugle thought *Somnambulist* was a comedy classic, the world did not agree.

Clay Men, however, was different. Even its creators were surprised when the film was picked up by fledgling company ZFA, who distributed it across German fleapits. The result was a mixed success. Those who loathed *Clay Men* saw only its all-too-apparent flimsiness. Those who loved it, mistook it for art.

"I didn't understand *Clay Men*," roared the critic from the *Holstenslava Gazette*, "but, my God, it's one of the best damn films I've ever seen."

The reviewer for the *Holstenslava Telegraph* was more succinct, writing simply: "I didn't understand *Clay Men*."

Amidst the ambivalence of early film journalists, Vincent Mugle, despondent that his painting career was, to be polite, going nowhere, had fallen in with a bunch of chicken-worshippers. This explained the ever-increasing moments when he was "out somewhere". His brain, too, seemed to be "out somewhere". Although artistic immortality had once been his aim, he no longer cared about leaving a mark upon this world; it already seemed blemished enough. So, he snuck out at night and performed various rituals with his new friends, the chicken-worshippers. These rituals mainly involved dancing naked in a cave with chickens. Eventually, Mugle sold his soul to the dark god Lord Poulet, in the hopes that he would gain the artistic immortality he once craved. But, like the more secular conmen of showbusiness today, the dark Lord did nothing for Mugle's career. He was still a bad painter. Instead, Vincent had to content himself with designing the cardboard sets for films like *Clay Men*, a delegation that inspired natural resentment, and didn't go unnoticed by the poor man's mother, who always thought a good carpet-layer had been lost to the arts.

Even when *Clay Men* drew praise, neither he nor his mother were mollified. Insult was added to injury when Mugle found out that his chicken-worshipping pals were just a bunch of phoneys who used their nefarious activities as a cover for poultry smuggling. Still, Vincent wanted to immortalise his new friends and their novel ideas in a film that would also expose them as the dull-witted chicken enthusiasts that they really were. Spurning, who would film just about anything, complied. The resultant feature, *Chicken Dance* (1920), is a curious mess: Two-and-a-half hours of bare-bottomed dancing with fowl.

Nevertheless, by then, *Clay Men* had received an all-important US release. This astounded everyone, especially the Americans, who hated it. A crowd of Californians even campaigned for the film to be banned when it crept its way into a major Los Angeles theatre (or theater as they spell it there). They claimed that clay monsters were "un-American".

"What do they know?" Spurning would splutter. "They're only offended because they didn't think of it themselves."

Mozella had other ideas. "They hate us because we stink."

TWENTY-SEVEN

Despite the Americans' indifference to *Clay Men*, they still went to watch it in droves. Indeed, the film was so profitable that Mozella, Spurning and Mugle were invited to Hollywood by revered movie mogul Louis Sedgewick, who wanted them to produce similar morbid efforts.

Suddenly, there was business in fantasy, and Mozella's strange countenance proved to be of greater curiosity than Larry "The Smirk" Valvadore, Hollywood's then-reigning prince. Nicknamed "The Smirk" because he smirked a lot, Larry had broken into pictures with *The Smirk* (1921), in which his smiling features won the hearts of the world. Although *Return of the Smirk* was rush-released to theatres the following year, Mozella had, by then, become the bigger box office draw. ("The Smirk" ultimately felt so dejected by Hollywood that, one day, back in '28, he wandered to the Pacific, and kept on walking. "I'd like to think he is still smirking somewhere," said Louis Sedgewick by means of tribute.)

When the three creatives behind *Clay Men* first slouched their way to Hollywood back in 1921, Elizabeth did not wish to join them. "Never again," was all she said, albeit repeatedly. She'd been so traumatized by the filming of her first, and last, motion picture that she returned to guide hedgehogs across Eckhorn Road. Spurning didn't seem too put out, and Mozella would return for his one true love later.

Meanwhile, Mozella and Spurning frittered away Sedgewick's money on a series of pictures that were wholly indifferent to Hollywood's usual fare. In *The Man with Twenty Fingers* (1923), for instance, Mozella plays a man with sixteen fingers and four thumbs on each hand—and those hands have a penchant for murder . . .

Chicken Freak (1924) sees Mozella playing a lowly circus janitor, who is forced to don animal costumes in order to become a performer. Unfortunately, the animal costumes take over . . .

It was as if the two men were tearing out their pasts and laying them to rest on celluloid. The spectre of Elizabeth still lay between them, of course, but this barbed indifference only seemed to fuel their work. They loved each other. They hated each other.

In *The Men Who Loved and Hated Each Other* (1925), two romantic rivals (played by Mozella and Spurning) try to kill each other—with hilarious results. Eventually, they transform their bungled murder attempts into a stage act that brings them fame and fortune. This cathartic treatment summed up the working relationship of director and star.

Another typical example of this early output is *The Man with Long Legs* (1925), in which Mozella falls in love with a woman several feet taller than himself. As she can't stand short men, Mozella chops off another man's legs and has them sewn to his own in an effort to woo her. Returning from the operation, however, he is devastated to find the girl of his dreams in the arms of a dwarf. Madness ensues . . . Elizabeth had always been taller than Mozella (at five foot eight, Mozella was probably the tallest dwarf in the world). This film was a way of easing those insecurities.

Mozella never stopped loving the "Hedgehog Lady". Once he'd established himself as a "kind of star", he returned to Holstenslava in 1931, and knelt before her on Eckhorn Road. Then he stood up again because he had knelt on a hedgehog and it prickled his knee. Then he proposed to her (Elizabeth, not the hedgehog).

With tears in her eyes, Elizabeth said no. Then she changed her mind and said yes. Then no. Then, reasoning that there were worse things than living in a Hollywood castle with a skull-headed actor, she said yes again. After all, she couldn't see herself walking hedgehogs forever. The pair fell in love eventually. And, for a while, happiness was their captor.

The same could not be said for Vincent Mugle, who left the movie business in 1947. Shortly afterwards, he died in a mysterious explosion at his LA condo. No one knows how the fire started; the only thing that didn't burn was the artist's final painting—a frenzied blaze of oils entitled *Flames*. It became the only artwork Mugle ever sold. Today, *Flames* hangs on a rich man's wall where, below it, guests in fancy frocks cram fish eggs into their faces and laugh at jokes they don't understand. Said one critic of *Flames*: "It is almost prophetic."

Similarly disillusioned, Max Spurning retired from the industry after a terrible car crash in which he lost his chin. Until his death in 1956, he sat alone in his villa, immersed in alcoholism and stamp-collecting, wearing a strap-on chin. *The Man with the Strap-On Chin* was a highly touted project that would reunite Spurning and Mozella. Sadly, it was never made, though a script was written, and used to add warmth to some producer's fireplace.

Following Elizabeth's death from natural causes in January '53, Mozella, too, hid himself away; retreating in his mind, back to his glory days, when he lived with his one true love . . .

TWENTY-EIGHT

Morbius and Elizabeth were married in 1933. For the remainder of the decade, they lived in a castle atop the Hollywood Hills. This was Mozella's "Golden Age"—an era that lasted until his popularity waned in the mid-1940s, when he was forced to find cheaper lodgings: the apartment where he still resided in 1967 (the castle was knocked down in 1948 to make way for a car wash).

Back in the 1930s, however, Mozella—who'd always envisioned life as a great romance—could live out his dreams for real. Each morning he'd sweep into Elizabeth's room with a specially prepared breakfast. He would then try in vain to capture her loveliness on canvas, before serenading her at the harmonium. Little did he know that Elizabeth hated organ music. Still, his career was going well.

No longer was he paid for things he didn't want to do. On any given day, he could be a pirate, pillaging flaming villages; a musketeer, rescuing damsels from a scoundrel's embrace; a detective, scouring the moorland for clues; or one of Poe's tortured souls, wandering forlorn across a mouldering set.

But, of course, the '30s were the years of his classic horror films: Grand, opulent, artful works that sprang from the literature of his dreaming youth. Throughout this period, Mozella was a great star; so great that he was billed by surname only, an honour that not even "The Smirk" was reduced to, and one previously only bestowed to that great actress, Garbles, whose first name now escapes me.

Louis Sedgewick was so pleased with Mozella's work that, one day, the mogul led his star to a fancy, ostentatious automobile, parked in the studio lot. "Nice, isn't it?" Louis grinned. "Do you know what kind of car this is?"

Mozella nodded. "A red one."

"That's right," said Louis, dragging Mozella over to a less flashy model. "You can have this one if you like. And I'll have the . . . er . . . the red one."

As Mozella had a lifelong distrust of "infernal machines", and never learned to drive anyway, the gesture was quite useless. Instead, the studio eventually got together and presented Mozella with a back-projection screen of fuzzy, rolling roads and a tin chassis without wheels. This way, the star could take imaginary drives whenever he wanted—a conclusion that seemed to suit everyone.

Ah, those were the days.

In the wild, weird world of Morbius Mozella, graveyards had never looked so beautiful, and the dead found life again. Man found something to cower from within his true self, and scientists believed that mating chimps with girls would obviously create a superior race. And the villain was always traced, by the bland leading man, back to his secret lair—which, being a huge castle, never looked quite so secret.

But yes. Happy days.

TWENTY-NINE

Hollywood, 1967.

Waking from his haze, Mozella shakes the nightmares from his brain. Although hindsight illuminates the times he's been remembering as his most contented days, he didn't feel that way when living them.

A photo of Benny Miller lies tattered on the floor. The comedian had presented it to Mozella on the first day of shooting *Benny Miller vs the Vampire Man*. Today, thank God, is the final day.

"If awful movies can reach completion," Mozella sighs, "then why, oh why can't I?"

The photo is signed by the hand of Miller's secretary and reads: *Hey, Mozella! Easy on the mayo! Good luck to you, Benny Miller.*

"Good luck," Mozella spits, threading an older, happier movie onto the projector. Soon, the ghosts of Max Spurning, Vincent Mugle and Elizabeth shimmer on the walls. Not just the walls of his shabby dwelling, but the walls of his true home: the one that lies behind his eyes.

"Life is but a dream," Mozella sings to himself. *And reality is a sad, damp thing that swallows our dreams whole.*

When the final reel flickers to black, Mozella looks to his wife in her box. "I only made movies so that you'd notice me," he whispers. "But you never really cared for films."

Overcome by darkness and dust, he leaves the spools to rot and his memoirs unfinished.

It is time to go to work. Again.

THIRTY

*Hollywood, 1967. The last day of shooting **Benny Miller vs the Vampire Man**.*

When Mozella arrives on set, Miller, Sharona and the director are already there. This is unusual—though it's not because they have some renewed vigour for work; they simply never went home from the party last night.

Benny Miller's nose is red and dripping with traces of white powder. His eyes are wide and darting. Sharona sits on a cardboard tombstone, bent beneath her toosh, staring silently into the studio gloom. The director lies slumped at Sharona's feet, heavy-lidded and drooling.

"Ah, Mozella!" Benny strides forward. "Finally, we can get to work!"

The director groans. Sharona sniffs.

Miller clasps Mozella round the shoulders. "I've had some ideas. This picture is about as funny as a kid with cancer. And I know what the problem is. There's too much of *you*, and too little of *me*."

Mozella peers up at his co-star, whose fingers are digging into his shoulders, close to snapping bone.

"Okay," Miller shouts, shoving Mozella aside. "Here's the new ending: I come in with this gun I found, and blast everybody away." The comedian lifts a shotgun from the prop table and waves it around his head.

The director shuffles to his feet. "But, Benny," he whimpers. "That doesn't make sense."

Miller glares at him. "What do you know, pipsqueak? It's the American way." He points the gun at the director and starts making *pow-pow* noises with his slimy lips. Then he pulls the trigger.

A sharp, loud blast echoes as the director explodes in a pulpy red mess.

"Shit," says Miller. "I didn't know this was real."

Sharona screams. "Aaaaarrrgghhh!"

"Oh, *now* you're screaming, baby," Miller turns the gun on the blood-spattered actress. "Easy on the mayo, bitch!"

He pulls the trigger. Sharona stops screaming and thuds to the floor. There's a gushing crimson mush where her head used to be.

"That's some haircut you got there." Shaking, Miller turns to Mozella. But the elder actor is gone.

Out on the sidewalk, Mozella hears a third and

final gunshot from within the studio walls. He's had enough of outsized egos for one day.

Returning to his apartment, he scoops Elizabeth into his arms and steps out through the humid air.

Turning his back on Hollywood, and all its twinkling filth, he continues walking long into the night, until he fades, like all good shadows in the dark.

EPILOGUE

Editorial, by Ed Lewton, for **Scream Screen** *magazine's "Morbius Mozella Special". Halloween 1967. "And now—at last—the Morbius Mozella Story!"*

The first film I saw, or at least remember seeing, was Morbius Mozella in *Escape from Count Casling's Castle* (1931). I wasn't scared—I was *fascinated*. From then on, I caught every Mozella movie I could.

I hated school. And I hated Mondays. The thrill of staying up late on a Friday or Saturday night to watch a Mozella offering on TV became the highlight of my week. I lived for these movies; they were twilights that swallowed me gladly, sparing me from reality, keeping Monday at bay. I longed to exist there forever, and all the excitement surrounding them could be issued to me in the breath of one magic word: *Mozella*.

Everything about these films appealed: from the demented poetry of the lyrical dialogue, to the artful direction and production design. They presented lost worlds, which opened before me: a haunted nirvana, a grey oasis where Good always vanquished Evil—just like a fairy tale. But, most of all, it was the unusual portrayals of my idol, Mozella, that I fell in love with. His monsters employed thought, his demons possessed soul, and his madmen held logic. These were characters you could *feel* for.

These films helped shape my imagination, and I would not be a writer today without them. For that I am eternally grateful. I followed Mozella's career, watching it grow and plummet alongside the rhythms of my own life. As a child, I would describe his oeuvre as "fun monster flicks". As a teenager and adolescent, these films were a mirror to the development of my own angst-ridden soul. And now, as an adult, I can enjoy them for all my former reasons, and also admire their importance in the development of cinema itself (as angst-ridden as ever was my teenage soul).

The majesty of those early movies I grew up with gave way to inevitable decline, and Mozella was often reduced to a parody of himself, appearing in such dreck as *Curse of the Yellow Banana* (1952). Nevertheless, the films were still entertaining, and I enjoyed them just as much—Mozella being of far more interest to me than the slick, overly glossed product Hollywood will perennially be keen on churning out.

Following the abysmal failure of the autobiographical *Hedgehog Man* (1954), however, Mozella seemed to vanish. So, it was with great excitement that I heard the great man was resuming his career with the ill-fated *Benny Miller vs the Vampire Man* (set for release this Christmas). This resurgence inspired me to tell, for the first time, the Mozella story.

Although I was raised by the glowing late-night box, my parents always looked down on these "bogy stories" of Mozella's, wishing I could find pleasure in "normal" fare, like Westerns or war movies (not seeming to realise that these were more unpleasant and violent than Mozella's gentle fantasies). What I perceived to be my parents' miscomprehension was really a general feeling entertained by all the world but me, it seemed.

Mozella is no longer popular in popular culture. The Horror film, and Mozella's contribution to it, has always been an unjustly neglected area of cinema. Despite an audience popularity that was once worldwide, fellow actors, filmmakers and critics remain sniffy regarding Mozella's work. Biased as I am, I've always believed these opinions to be unfounded. To make the unbelievable believable, as Mozella did time and again, is a true achievement. After all, isn't that what cinema is all about? Making the unbelievable believable? I hope this tribute will both inspire reappraisal in the reader's own heart for Mozella's often glorious efforts, and endure, at least, as a testament to his memory.

Whilst compiling this special, I was allowed access onto the set of *Benny Miller vs the Vampire Man*, and I could, finally, see my hero at work. These observations formed the periphery of my story, and fully convinced me that a *Scream Screen* special on Mozella was long overdue. I felt a heartfelt duty to impart the truth of this remarkable yet forgotten artist.

In the late summer of this year, I finally came face to face with my idol. Word had gotten around about my project and Mozella was initially interested in how it would take shape. As a result, I was invited to his modest Hollywood home, where a series of nightlong discussions evolved on his life and work. I also carried out several interviews with every survivor of the Mozella story I could find. Their numbers were few, their memories dim; and I thank them for their precious time.

One thing that became clear during my discussions with those who knew Mozella during his life is that, despite being close, they never *felt* close. No one really knows this man. He seems to haunt life as a shadow, yet a shadow in whose darkness we continue to be enthralled. Hopefully this tribute will prove the fullest attempt to give character to the shadow. Regrettably, the majority of my interviewees wished to remain as shadows themselves: anonymous—a wish I have duly respected.

I was also allowed access to Mozella's unpublished memoirs, which he was writing at the time of our meeting. These avowed an unparalleled view into the actor's life, especially the early years of which nothing was really known. Until now. I have allowed Mozella's own prose to grace the pages only when I felt my own words fell short of such eloquence. Indeed, this precious manuscript was invaluable in my efforts to convey the truth and feeling of Mozella's tortuous life. Who knows, one day it might be published in its entirety?

I have also gleaned valuable, often contradictory, information from studio records and sources, both from my own vast collection of film memorabilia and Mozella's personal artefacts, which I was, again, allowed unconditional access to. Among the latter, I was pleased to discover the unreleased audio memoirs of Mozella's friend and fellow filmmaker, Max Spurning. Transcribed excerpts from these recordings can be found in these pages.

Mozella also owned prints of many of his old movies, which he screened for me in the dubious comfort of his apartment. Many of these are rare, some considered lost, and it was both a treat and a revelation to view them with their star, whose illuminating comments were of utmost interest.

My observations of Mozella at home during this period also form an insightful backbone to this work. I found the hospitality of the great man to be warm, gracious and, above all, odd. After all, not everyone keeps their dead wife propped up in a box against the living room wall, do they?

Ultimately, I formed an impression of a man who was no longer in control; so far away did he live in his own little world. Indeed, he would often forget I (and the world) was there.

Now, with the news of Mozella's recent disappearance—amid what has come to be known as the "Poverty Row Massacre" (as mysterious as anything from the Master's own films)—interest in the actor has yet again risen like a vampire from the tomb. And hence this tome, this man-made monster, is finally permitted life.

Life has always fascinated me: we are each given this precious gift, and yet each of us, no matter who we are, or where we come from, choose to do something totally different with it. Yet, from the lives of others, we take inspiration that helps carry us along our own destined paths. I hope you find as much inspiration within the darkened recesses of Mozella's life as I have myself. I like to believe we became friends, the shadow and I.

And I miss him.

ABOUT THE AUTHOR

A lifelong lover of movies and monsters, **Stephen Mosley** played the monster in the movie *Kenneth*. His other acting credits include the eponymous paranormal investigator of *Kestrel Investigates*; the shady farmer, James, in *Contradiction*; a zombie in *Zomblogalypse*; and a blink-and-you'll-miss-it appearance opposite Sam Neill in *Peaky Blinders*.

As well as being the author of *Klawseye: The Imagination Snatcher of Phantom Island*; *The Boy Who Loved Simone Simon*; and an upcoming biography of Christopher Lee, *The Loneliness of Evil* (from Midnight Marquee Press), Stephen is one half of the music duo Collinson Twin and has contributed to the books *Masters of Terror; Dead or Alive: British Horror Films 1980-1989; 70s Monster Memories; Unsung Horrors; A Celebration of Peter Cushing;* and *Son of Unsung Horrors.*

His film articles have appeared in magazines *The Dark Side, Midnight Marquee, We Belong Dead,* and *Multitude of Movies,* while his short stories have been included in such anthologies as *Dracula's Midnight Snacks* and *Zombie Bites.*

Please visit: www.stephenmosley.net

Copyright © Stephen Mosley 2021

Stephen Mosley